ALIEN FREQUENCY
STELLAR FLASH BOOK ONE

NEIL A. HOGAN

Space Fiction Books

Get your Free eBook!

Captain Victoria Heartness takes command of the newly built Stellar Flash, and heads on a routine mission to investigate a possible First Contact situation.

But, with the strange effects of the new frequency, the disappearance of a crew member, and now a mutiny, she must use all her wits to escape and bring everyone back to Frequency Zero.

Can she save her ship and crew before her unstable pilot destroys the world?

Get a free copy of the Stellar Flash prequel
The Pilot here:

www.StellarFlash.com

Names, characters, places, businesses, products, situations and events portrayed in this title are fictitious, and any similarities to anyone living or dead is purely coincidental.

Copyright © 2017, 2018 by Neil A. Hogan
All rights reserved

No part of this release may be transmitted or reproduced in any form without the express permission of the author and publisher, except for fair use in relation to reviews.

Published by Space Fiction Books, Melbourne
www.SpaceFictionBooks.com

For Mum and Dad

Contents

Prelude	7
Introduction	9
Chapter 1: Saturn Space Station X-1a	10
Chapter 2: Frequency One	25
Chapter 3: Discovery	40
Chapter 4: Contingencies	46
Chapter 5: Take Me To Your Leader	54
Chapter 6: Stuck	62
Chapter 7: Breach	67
Chapter 8: A Gift in Time	79
Chapter 9: Stellar Breeze	95
Chapter 10: Mashbug	104
Chapter 11: Puppy's Lament	110
Chapter 12: Geo's Metrics	115
Chapter 13: Murder on the Stellar Flash	122
Chapter 14: We Come in Pieces	139
Chapter 15: Clouded	144
Chapter 16: Released	150
Chapter 17: The Three Bodies Problem	154
Chapter 18: Evolution	160
Chapter 19: The One is All and the All are One	168
Chapter 20: Torus and Events	191
Chapter 21: First Contact	204
Postlude	208

Prelude
2133/08/17/11:30 Monday

The binary suns blazed in the brown and purple sky as the space-suited Captain Jonathan Hogart wrestled with the mushroom and bug-like alien on the ramp.

With his bioelectrical signal now accelerated, the aliens had detected him and his crew, and were on the attack. Hogart thought his nanite suit's strength-enhancing properties would have had himself out of this sticky situation in no time, but the mushroom-bugs had other ideas, and now he was being bounced back to his crew.

Not far away, his first officer had his own problems. Looking much like an overgrown urchin, Spiney had been spinning and throwing bug attacks off with his spines as fast as they could jump him. But they had worked out that simply lifting him with their antennae would stop him from moving, and he had momentarily hung helpless between a group of the mushroom-bugs, before they had dropped him and jumped on him.

The third member of their team, Cuddly, a caterpillar-like alien with sucker legs, had curled up like a tire, hoping to avoid the fight while his translator belt continued working on the language.

Now the three of them were pinned under so many hard antennae-flicking bodies that their nanite suits were struggling to stop them from being crushed. If the nanites failed in this deadly atmosphere, it would be all over.

"Not the best start to our first mission together," yelled Hogart.

"I guess it's time to say it then," Spiney's translator stuttered.

"No. No. I will not say it."

"I will," said Cuddly. "I just finished the translation."

Through the chattering of the bugs, they heard a scratching sound coming from Cuddly. He'd recreated the bugs' speaking alert, and the creatures stopped moving, waiting for the message. Cuddly then sent a signal to his nanite suit to create antennae, similar to the bug on top of him. Five antennae grew out from an area not held by one of the bugs, made some complicated twisting movements, then stopped.

"Did you say it?" groaned Hogart.

"I said it. Our only option."

"I see," said Spiney.

Introduction

It is the year 2133, just one hundred years after Alien Shift. Humanity can now perceive the trillions of alien races that live in the galaxy, having finally increased their frequency speed to Zero. Now a member of the Interdimensional Coalition, humanity works with alien races from all over the universe on Flash ships, exploring realities on higher level frequencies, and instigating First Contact with new alien races. The Stellar Flash Frequency Ship is the newest addition to the universal mission.

Chapter 1:
Saturn Space Station X-1a
2133/08/17/10:00 Monday

Saturn Space Station X-1a spun silently on the day side of its namesake planet, just above the rings. A massive feat of human and alien engineering, built by robots, aliens, humans and nanites, and about a hundred kilometers long, the multiple-spoked orbital base was equipped with ship repair systems, xenobiology research sections, a hospital, an archive, and plenty of restaurants, bars and entertainment to keep any visiting aliens busy.

Not only that, there were enough redundant systems that almost any being would survive a collision, if one of the billions of rocks circling Saturn decided to go its own way. While not impenetrable, the base was close to indestructible.

X-1a was the assembly point for any humans and aliens planning a trip to another frequency. A security measure to reduce the possibility of any unauthorized being knowing the exact location of Earth, until first contact had been established successfully, or the rejected planet had been heavily quarantined.

A bright light appeared briefly in one of the hundreds of windows of Ring One, illuminating the under-construction support struts of the soon to be completed Ring Two.

A female face looked out the window onto the rings

and the slowly moving moon Cassini before moving back inside, as more flashes appeared.

The window quickly brightened further before dimming again, with more faces looking out the window. Purple faces, glutinous faces and six-eyed faces all looked out at the wonder of Saturn, before turning around.

Inside, hundreds of aliens had flashed in from around the galaxy and across the frequencies for a very important meeting. They turned to look at the closed door to the room. One more person was expected.

Outside, in the silver and black corridor with tastefully patterned blue carpet, Captain Jonathan Hogart stood, staring at the doors, waiting for the flashes of appearing aliens to die down.

Hogart was a pinkish-white, muscular man in his early 40s, with short dark-brown hair, and a sparkle in his eyes that suggested he was always about to make a joke. He looked up at one of the nearby security cameras and grinned. "Let's see how I look."

He pressed his temple, activating his mind-view system, accessing the camera signal of himself. He turned slightly for a view of his back. "Good enough for the viewers, I guess." He shrugged and mentally switched it off.

Straightening his front shirt and taking a deep breath, Hogart made to push open the doors, when a large blue humanoid alien with a thick beard came up the corridor barreling towards him.

"Captain Hogart!" the alien gasped as he ran up to him and squinted, pushing his face so closely that his beard touched Hogart's chin. "Yes, it is you, isn't it? Can I skip this bit?"

"Sorry?" asked Hogart, stepping back a little to give himself more space. As the alien attempted to move closer Hogart held up his hands. "Human personal space, well, American at any rate. Can you stand there, please?"

The alien gasped, evidently short of breath, and nodded. "Of course, captain, I'm sorry."

"Who are you?"

The being straightened himself, his overweight belly struggling to remain confined in his tight Flash-issued trousers, and announced proudly, "I am your new Storyteller. Jorjarar. Please to meet you." Then, as if shortcutting any possible further conversation, he said bluntly. "I don't want to go in there." Jorjarar pointed at the door, then made a cross shape with his flat hands.

Hogart suddenly remembered. The Storytellers. They had one on every flash ship, linked to everyone's thoughts while in other frequencies. As retaining memories between frequencies was impossible for many from Frequency Zero, most of them relied on the Storytellers to remember for them.

"Pleased to meet you, Jorjarar," said Hogart. "I thought you'd want to record the big introduction of senior crew, and then my captain's speech. Big day. Important occasion and all that."

Jorjarar briefly looked positively horrified at the thought, then changed his expression to one of obsequiousness, rubbing his hands together slightly.

Hogart knew he would have to watch out for this one.

"Oh, Captain. It takes me awhile to get set up, and I should be on the ship ready to link to everyone's thoughts the moment they're on board. Just give me a quick overview as to what will happen in there, and I'll be able to add your personal reports into that section when I get back."

Hogart looked down at him. No one except the Storytellers could be so bold as to request not to attend a ceremonial meeting, especially one in which *he* gave a speech. But he decided to allow it this once. After all, at the end of the day, the Storyteller's report was the one that mattered, and he didn't want any negativity creeping into any description of him.

Hogart sighed. "Well, Jorjarar, I'm going to go on stage, give a quick talk about how wonderful this all is, introduce the main crew members one by one to everyone, then we'll all flash to the ship. I'd say a twenty minute meeting? A bit of banter. That sort of thing."

"Perfect," said Jorjarar. "I'll flash to the ship now and get ready. One more thing. This meeting bit. Will there be any dramatic situation that would lead into the experience on the ship?"

Hogart raised his eyebrows. "Well, I hope not. It's just a meeting. If you don't want to experience it, start with us on the ship in the next section."

"Great idea, sir. Yes, thank you." Jorjarar pressed a button on the flash band on his pudgy blue arm, and disappeared with a flash of white light.

Hogart sighed. He really didn't like the idea of Storytellers getting into his skull to record his experiences. But it was part of the rules now.

He checked himself again, then pushed the heavy doors slowly open with both hands and strode purposely through the crowd of aliens towards the podium. The chatter of hundreds of translators died down as many of the aliens realized that the meeting was about to begin.

He looked about admiringly, as he strode to the other side of the room, at all the non-humanoid shaped aliens who had endeavored to make the flash uniforms work for them. Not many, but those with at least vaguely humanoid bodies had been able to make an effort.

"Well, team," he began as he stepped up onto the stage, his voice echoing in the wide area. "This is it."

"Ahem," said a voice. Hogart turned and saw Captain Victoria Heartness standing near the back curtain of the stage. A short, thin, almost elfin woman with long blonde hair, she made a show of looking exasperated. "I know you're desperate to take over, but can I just give my farewell speech?"

Hogart looked down his nose at her, squinting, getting into character. He was going to have fun with this. "My God. Really? A speech? How long will that take?"

A number of aliens in the front row rustled, rumbled and sparked. Was he insulting her?

Then Hogart grinned, spreading his arms wide. "My dear Heartness, darling. Of course you can. You took great care of some of the crew here, according to the reports, and I wouldn't have it any other way."

Hogart stepped aside and waved her to the podium, a condescending smile on his face. Heartness raised her eyebrows, then gave a quiet 'humph'. With her blue suit freshly pressed, it looked like she wasn't going to let her moment be taken away from her. She turned to face the crowd of aliens with a beaming smile.

"My wonderful crew." She reached out her arms like she wanted to hug them all. "Thank you very much for coming with me on so many voyages to Frequency One. I've been promoted to Admiral and..."

So, that was the surprise she had been hinting at, thought Hogart. He quickly interrupted with some heavy clapping, nodding at the crowd of aliens as though encouraging them to clap, too. Of course, most of the aliens didn't know what nodding was, or why he was making those strange banging noises with his upper appendages.

Heartness gave him a stern look and he stopped. "...and so, with a breaking heart I hereby pass the Stellar Flash and all you incredible aliens onto the er... infamous Captain Jonathan Hogart."

"Excellent," said Hogart, and made to step up to the podium.

"I'm not finished," said Heartness.

Hogart rolled his eyes.

Heartness smiled at the assembled aliens. "I know that our adventures in One were quickly forgotten when we returned to Zero, so I have reread the reports of them and can confirm that you all did very well, in all the situations we were up against. There were a number of times when our lives were in danger, and everyone helped to save us from whatever it was that we had needed saving from."

Hogart gave a slight clap to the aliens, who stood there silently, probably wondering what this was all about. He quickly scanned them. So many colors and shapes, some his mind couldn't even define. It looked like he was going to be the only human on board. Oh well. He spotted the translucent gelatinous forms of a couple of xenosexuals. Hmm. That could be interesting.

"...and so," Heartness had been speaking and Hogart had missed it. He had already read most of her speech, though. She'd probably just finished the bit about welcoming the new crew members. "Captain Hogart will finish the mission we started on the mushroom-bug world. I only hope that he is more successful than me in bringing a First Contact situation to that planet."

Heartness then stepped aside from the lectern and Hogart almost leaped at it, turning to her.

"Thank you, Admiral Heartness. You did a great job, apparently. I wish you all the best in your endeavors."

Then he turned to the crowd again. "And another round of applause for Admiral Heartness's promotion." Just in case they missed it the first time. He was about to bow but thought better of it, especially as none of the aliens had joined him in applauding, though he did hear some clacking of something coming from up the back.

"Right team. You're now all part of MY crew. For the new recruits, you've read the specs, studied at our universities, and have seen her out of this station's windows. It's almost time to go on board the Stellar Flash."

He pulled out a piece of plastic with notes on it. "I've been through the ship's roster and there are six aliens I'd like on the Center Bridge. Admiral Heartness, and the officers before her, have all said these aliens exemplify what humanity is trying to achieve with its flash ships, and I'm very happy to announce my team here. If you can come to the stage when I call your name..."

Then he saw the names. He looked at the sheet and

blinked. How had he not noticed that before? He'd read their specs many times, but the names were always at the top, and it had been their personal profiles he had been more interested in.

An unscripted moment. His brow furrowed. How was he going to play this? Maybe he could show surprise?

It was Heartness's turn to grin.

Hogart looked at her with his eyebrows high. "These aren't their original alien names!" he said, almost choking. "These are nicknames you created for them!!!"

Heartness shrugged. "Some don't have names, and some names aren't translatable into any human language."

"But, I can't call an alien 'Puppy!'"

Heartness laughed. "He's been okay with it. I'm sure you'll be fine."

Hogart let his hand shake the plastic slightly, then changed his expression to indignation.

"These are all girly names! Other captains will think I'm some kind of girlyman!"

"It's not the name that's important, it's the judgement you give it. Give it affection, and it'll be alright."

"I don't have any of your feminine energy, and I'm not going to be affectionate with anyone." Hogart frowned.

"Hmm," Heartness put a finger to her chin pointedly, and looked at the curtains, as though dropping some gossip. "Well, a few girls I know have said that you can be quite affectionate."

Hogart looked taken aback at this.

"In any case," she continued, turning back to him.

"Things are different on the higher frequencies, captain. You may find yourself becoming more feminine."

"Over my dead body." He hmphed. Hmm. Had he gone too far with that one?

The noise of the alien crowd grew louder as everyone's translators were struggling to keep up with the exchange, and then discussions began when Hogart used the word 'dead.' It wasn't a word to be used in polite company. Best to get back to the script. He turned back to the waiting crowd.

"Alright, alright." Hogart lifted his hands to quieten them. "First up, Spiney."

A round, purplish figure with hundreds of spikes sticking out of its body, made a slapping sound that translated as 'yes' and waddled to the stage area. Hogart ducked and stepped back as one of the larger spines got a bit too close for comfort.

"You'll be my first officer," Hogart said, then looked back at his sheet.

"Puppy!" At the back, with plenty of space around him, a large greenish spider-like creature on twelve pole-like legs, raised its massive, almost flat, three-piece body, waved its wide circular head with six eyes, and began loping towards the stage. Many aliens were quick to get out of the way of him, while some just watched him step over them, staring with open mouths.

"Don't you just want to hug him," said Heartness, seeing Hogart's shocked look.

"I didn't realize he was so big!"

Puppy let out a long, purple tongue and his translator said, "That's what they all say." Then he closed one of his six eyes briefly. A wink?

Hogart almost laughed. "Ah, funny guy, are you? Good. I need people like you on the Center bridge. You'll be my security officer." He recognized the clicking of the alien's legs. So, it was Puppy that had been clapping.

He turned and whispered to Heartness, seriously. "Funny guys usually die first. How'd he make it through his tour of duty?"

"According to some reconstructed memories, he's only really funny between missions."

Hogart nodded, then looked at his sheet again. "Cud..dly," he glared at Heartness, who gave him a winning smile, then he turned back to the crowd. "My second officer and communications advisor." A large green caterpillar-like creature with many segments, a number of sucker-like legs on the front, and a much larger translator system around its middle, inched up to the stage.

Heartness leant over and whispered, "Cuddly is a bit shy. Make sure he gets lots of toilet breaks, and try not to mention it."

Hogart nodded and turned to Cuddly. "I heard you can channel beings as well. Can you teach me telepathy?"

"I'll do my best, sir," Cuddly's translator rasped.

"Great! Probably not this mission, but definitely soon!" Hogart looked at his sheet again. "Geo, the best mathematician in the fleet, and you're an astrophysicist too!"

A ball with many light-colored tear-drop shapes in various positions around it rolled down the middle of the room, the drops shifting around its body to accelerate. Then a drop shape flicked out, and Hogart could see two big black eyes, surrounded by hair, hiding in the middle of the ball. Geo held up a drop and put it down again. His way of greeting? He rolled up the steps and settled down next to Puppy.

"Alright," said Hogart. "Amy!" He looked for her in the crowd. "Stellar Flash is fitted with the latest in medical and repair systems for aliens and robots. But anything can happen in space, and if the system fails, Amy will step in. Our ship's doctor and astrobiologist."

A splashing, squelching sound began coming from the left, and a greenish, transparent blob of gelatinous material shifted through many of the other aliens, sliding between their legs, sliding over their shells and even briefly turning into a wall to quickly flow through a close group of plant aliens.

Hogart nodded appreciatively. One of the xenosexuals.

Amy made it to the stage, and immediately formed a human female shape with curves in almost all the right places, but with hair that seemed to drip rather than hang. She flipped it with her hand suggestively, then stood next to the other crew, squelching down into an amorphous blob. Hogart momentarily gaped before turning away.

Then he suddenly realized why she was called Amy and turned to Heartness. In a quiet, slightly strangled voice he said, 'as in Amoeba?"

Heartness winked.

Hogart grimaced, then looked at his sheet again. "And finally, Torus."

There was a flash, and suddenly a toroidal-shaped energy ball materialized on the stage. "Thank you Captain Hogart," it vibrated. "It is with great pleasure that I accept your invitation to join your crew."

Hogart smiled. "Torus will be our engineer and technician and be a backup for everyone else."

"That's only six," whispered Heartness. "There are eight stations, so you need one more! Where's your pilot?"

"Yes," said Hogart, mysteriously, continuing his speech to the crowd. "The Stellar Flash is in need of a pilot. It can flash to any location in this and other universes, of course, but someone needs to drive it once we get there. I will be giving most of this responsibility to the AI. However, we will sometimes need a backup pilot and I will then contact other crew on board. Let's plan for a guest pilot of the week!"

"Hogart." Heartness sounded worried. "You can't. The Stellar Flash is a conscious entity on another level. The AI can operate it, but it can't fully integrate with it. At some point you're going to need someone who has a similar consciousness."

Hogart leant over to her and urgently whispered back. "Since the issue with your previous pilot, Earth has asked me to find a way around having to have a permanent one, as the only real benefit to merged consciousnesses is slightly faster reaction times."

Heartness looked thoughtfully at him, shifting back into playing the role again, her voice loud enough for all to hear. "Hmm. Well. As long as they're chosen fairly. Don't just invite all the pretty females in return for favors."

Hogart looked at her with a pretend shocked expression on his face. "Would I do that?"

Then he turned back again to the hundreds of alien crew members that stood patiently, listening and translating. "So, what do you think? I'm sure there are some aliens here who want a go at being a pilot. Let's see a show of hands and err, tentacles, tarsus, leaves, whatever you have, if this is something that would interest you."

A few of the aliens near the back spat in the air, made a hoot sound or flashed various colors. Hogart nodded. At least he had their attention.

He looked over at his Center crew on the stage. "Well team, are you excited? Ready to take us all to Frequency One for our first mission? I'm sure you are!"

There was, of course, no real reaction. Perhaps Spiney's spines changed color a little. Perhaps Amy's translucent body shifted a few molecules or Torus' energy field flickered more, but there weren't any sounds from the translators, and they weren't programmed to translate alien body language anyway.

Hogart walked in front of his new alien crew members and looked them up and down seriously, then remembered Jorjarar, realizing now that he agreed with him. If he could have avoided having to go through these twenty minutes of posturing and posing, he would have. Unfortunately, it was a crucial part of the whole launch, and helped get them continued support from various government departments, private enterprises and charity organizations on Earth. Not to mention their fan clubs.

None of the alien races did anything similar on their worlds, but they were happy to attend, and the viewers back home loved it. He knew that this would be broadcast to billions of people in the Solar System, though he would have left on the mission before the signal actually got anywhere, and even then it would be edited into a one-minute news story on people's mind viewers for them to decide whether to watch or not.

He briefly touched his temple and checked the time via his mind view, then turned and gave Heartness a knowing wink. She had been playing along with his antics, giving the viewers something to talk about. The wink was to let her know he was about to finish. He turned back to the rustling crowd.

"These are your superior officers." He pointed his hand at the beings next to him. "Please treat them with the respect they deserve. Please also feel free to ask them for help if you need it. For many of you who have never been to Frequency One before, you can contact any of them if you need any help through the transitions."

He looked back over at Heartness. "Any last words?"

Heartness shook her head. "I think you've covered everything. Now you've got about 15 minutes to get to the ship!"

Hogart pretended to look horrified. "Gaah!"

He quickly rolled up his plastic info sheet and checked all his pockets. They'd tried to work out what would be a great thing to do to get a heading on some of the news feeds. 'New Captain Almost Misses Launch Window,' might get some attention. "New Captain is Rude to Admiral' probably not so much. Still, any publicity is good publicity, he thought. "Alright team, it's time. Let's get to the Stellar Flash."

Heartness gave Hogart a grin, her face showing that she was relieved that was over. "Wish you all the best Captain." She saluted him.

Hogart saluted back. "I wish you all the best too, Admiral."

Then, as if on cue, all the aliens in the room pressed, flicked, activated or otherwise engaged their address relocation systems, and materialized in their designated rooms on the Stellar Flash, their personal effects having been transported there earlier that day.

Hogart tapped the bright silver flash band on his wrist and also disappeared.

As the flashes in the meeting hall died down, and the light of the environment faded back to normal, Admiral Victoria Heartness looked about the empty room. Her tour of duty between the frequencies was over. She could now take that desk job that she'd just been offered and manage many of the ships from afar. "Well then," she said sadly, then strode purposefully out.

She was sure her new duties would have nothing to do with the Stellar Flash.

She had no idea how wrong that would turn out to be.

Chapter 2
Frequency One

Captain Jonathan Hogart flashed to the bridge of his new ship and saw that his crew were already at their stations. "Good work!" He looked around appreciatively. Heartness had given him a brief tour weeks ago, but it was like taking a test drive in someone else's vehicle. There was that feeling of it finally being yours. He couldn't stop himself from grinning. The best spacecraft in humanity's fleet, and he was the captain. What did his grandfather used to say? Ah, that was it. 'How awesome!'

The Stellar Flash was the latest in human technology, based on alien designs from the Interdimensional Coalition. The I.C. remained in Frequency Seven, and rarely had anything to do with the lower frequencies besides send some alien technology ideas to engineers in their dreams. When this information had begun appearing a few decades ago, engineers had quickly come up with new ways to utilize it, sending ideas via mind view to every other engineer on the planet.

The relocation technology utilized the electromagnatheric energy that existed in another level of reality, and allowed for instantaneous transportation of anyone and anything, anywhere in the universe. When it was finally understood that objects were not in a location or time, the location and time were part of the object, and that it was possible to superimpose the vibration of a new location and time on the current object's vibration within an isolation field, Earth became a utopia almost overnight.

With unlimited free energy, and no longer any need for any kind of costly public transportation system, an economy of time trading had quickly replaced money, as the expert you needed for absolutely anything, that also wanted your unique expertise in exchange, would be able to appear before you anywhere in the universe in minutes. The massive leap in technology had transformed the entire human race in under twelve months.

Of course, none of this could have happened if Alien Shift hadn't happened in 2033, allowing for the next generation of people to accept rapid and total change every minute. Previous generations wouldn't have been able to cope. Even Hogart, a homo galacticus human born near the end of the 21st century, was still coming to terms with the rapid leaps in technology every day.

Hogart thought about his ship. It was so completely different to what many had expected a future ship to be like. Many of the old files he'd read and gamevids he'd immersed in had predicted long rocket-like vehicles with wings and lines. No one would have ever thought they'd be flying around in something like the Stellar Flash.

The ship was quite nondescript. Completely functional, from a distance, it looked like a black triangle with a wide semisphere in the center. While the surface seemed to be some undefinable shade of shiny black, within the metal teemed billions of repair bots dealing with anything from radiation damage to metal fatigue.

On each flat corner of the triangular-shaped ship was an airlock that led along internal crisscrossing corridors leading to the center. Underneath the corners were three lights, and towards the center a much larger light. These helped with course adjustments as well as stabilizing the isolation field. The larger light also had many other uses and could be adapted to do just about anything.

The ship was big, a kilometer in length on each side, but Hogart knew it wasn't much bigger than a large 21st century shopping mall. And everything was on one level. No lifts, stairs or ladders to cause too many problems for any aliens.

Inside the semisphere above the large light was the Center, or bridge / command deck / observation room / control sphere, or whatever other captains, engineers or aliens called it, and it was encircled by a three-hundred-and-sixty-degree spherical screen that displayed the immediate outside of the triangular ship.

When the door to the Center closed behind Hogart, it was almost like they were on a small opaque floor with eight station stands floating in the vacuum of space, with a split, white energy column in the center. One section of the column through the floor and the other hanging from the ceiling.

The floor itself could be made transparent too, if needed, but Hogart found it to be a little disconcerting.

The Center was really designed for their alien crew. Humans preferred looking forward, and old ships used to only have a forward screen. Many aliens had advised that they couldn't see anything that was happening around the ship, so the Center had been built. Unfortunately, it was a bit uncomfortable for humans who only had eyes at the front, and Hogart knew he'd probably end up with neck ache if he had to keep looking around. He would rely on the crew to do that for him.

"AI?" he called.

There was a slight hum, and an image representing the AI formed in front of him. A fit Japanese woman of about thirty appeared. Long black hair, flawless skin, professional black suit, thin rimmed glasses, she looked more like a teacher than a state-of-the-art computer program. He guessed that the software adjusted to the user, and he'd always had a thing for Japanese culture. "AI. Are you ready to pilot this vessel?"

The AI froze for a moment, checking data, then reanimated. "Yes, Captain. Frequency One co-ordinates are set, and we can leave at any time."

Hogart turned to his crew of aliens. They were standing at their stations which were positioned in a circle of eight, facing outward towards the Center's surround screen walls. They all had some part of their bodies connected to their white screens - checking systems, monitoring crew, but not really doing much yet. The moment they arrived in Frequency One, they'd be busy.

"AI, activate flash drive."

In the surround screens, Saturn was slowly turning on the right, with the space station's massive wheel and half-complete spokes structure turning on the left. The Stellar Flash was orbiting just above the rings, with Saturn's icy moon Enceladus directly behind them.

Hogart looked in wonder at Saturn, and further out to the bright star in the distance that was Sol, the sun.

He so loved this system. Even though the plan was for a day trip and return to X-1a to report, he knew the risks. There was always the faint chance that he might not see his beloved Solar System again.

A hum began climbing as the Center's separated central column of white metal began glowing, and then along with an increasing vibration, arcs of electricity shot up and down it. The gap in the middle of the column began glowing, creating a bright white sphere that grew larger.

In moments the sphere expanded to fill the entire crew area, then expanded again, rushing through the entire ship.

Outside the ship, flashes spread across its surface like multiple lightning strikes, then the glow intensified, enveloping the entire structure in a spherical isolation and relocation field.

Moments later, the Stellar Flash disappeared, flickers of energy sparking across the vacuum where it used to be.

On the spherical screen inside, the white light of the energy sphere faded away to reveal a binary star system – a brown and purple planet solidifying next to it. The planet turned slowly on the right side of the screen, streaks of white, pink and blue in its atmosphere, small lakes of water peeking out from under the faint cloud cover.

Hogart was pleased to see that they had arrived at their destination. The binary star system occupied the exact same space/time as the Solar System but existed within the vibrational universe designated Frequency One.

Hogart had been given the explanation a few times, but it was different finally being here, on another channel of reality. He knew his Solar System was a turn of the dial away, but it was just the same as being an infinite number of kilometers away. Without this ship, he could never return to his own world.

As the ship stabilized, the crew flew into action, translators chattering, sending enquiries for information via their white panels.

"Thank you, AI," said Hogart. The hologram of the Japanese AI bowed and disappeared.

Hogart was beside himself. He'd finally made it to Frequency One, and it wasn't all that bad. In fact, his thoughts seemed clearer, and everything around him seemed more defined and easier to control.

He had heard that one of the side effects of experiencing another frequency was being able to manifest something out of thin air. He held out his hand and concentrated.

"Yes, sir?" asked Geo, thinking Hogart's hand was pointing towards him.

"Oh, sorry, Geo. I just thought I'd test a theory for myself and try to make something appear with my mind."

"I understand."

Hogart stared at his hand for a few seconds, but nothing happened.

He put it down again. "Oh well. No apple." He sighed. It must have been a myth. Or maybe it worked on a higher frequency. "Well, team, let's get down there."

"Two volunteers?" asked Spiney.

"Actually, I'd like you and Cuddly to come with me. I need Cuddly to work on finding a way to translate the language, and I need you to be my backup. I would have liked to bring Torus too, but I heard that this world is not really suitable for him during the daytime, and I need the others in the Center for this mission."

"Yes," agreed Torus. "The magnetic fields from these particular binary suns mean, without the protection of the Stellar Flash, I am unable to fully corporealize on the day side." Torus didn't sound apologetic, just stating a fact.

"Next time, Torus. Hopefully the next mission will be easier on you. Alright, Cuddly?"

"Let me just go to..." began Cuddly, and Hogart waved him off. He quickly inched through the Center doors and down the corridor to the waste disposal room.

Hogart strode around his new crew, getting a feel for being their captain. He could easily just give orders but he preferred a bit of conversation. He wasn't the sort of leader that usually followed the rule of 'don't give a reason'. All the aliens needed explanations, and their feedback on his decisions could be helpful. "While Cuddly is indisposed, can someone give me a run down? I know you've been here before, but I haven't. And I don't fully trust Frequency Zero reporting when most of our memories come back transformed. What can you tell me is there, right now?"

"Quick summary, sir," said Geo. "The planet's atmosphere is mainly hydrogen, nitrogen and carbon dioxide. There are a number of habitats on the planet, and a few of the buildings that the team visited last time look like they might be part of a school, though we didn't stay long enough to check them out. The indigenous population has a physiognomy that looks like something between what you would call a bug and fungi." Geo put one of his drops against his panels, and a hologram of one of the aliens appeared within the space between the ceiling and floor columns, slowly turning. It had a wide mushroom shape with five antennae sticking out of the top of one end of it. The antennae were colored and moved in complicated shapes.

"I thought the Stellar Flash lost everything when it returned to our frequency," said Hogart. "I only saw sketches."

"Everything is still here, it just can't be seen in Frequency Zero," said Puppy. "When you return to Frequency One, everything becomes accessible again."

Hogart nodded at Puppy. He guessed that if Puppy knew how to wink, he probably knows what nodding means. "Anything else?"

"Your first flash location will be a little bit further away from our original landing point," said Amy. "Use nanite suits, not force suits, as there is a chance of a force suit being detected by some of the more sensitive locals. Spiney can show you where they went last time."

"Thank you, team."

Hogart heard Cuddly inching himself back into the Center, smelling slightly of something like nail polish remover. Hogart thought best not to joke about it. He didn't want to start a diplomatic incident. Most of the aliens on the ship had engaged their nanite waste systems and didn't need to take regular toilet visits, but he understood that Cuddly's wastes were so corrosive that the nanite recycling systems couldn't cope with the process.

He made a mental note to make sure Cuddly was back on board with plenty of time.

"Alright Spiney, Cuddly, you're with me. The rest of you, keep an eye on us and, at the first sign of trouble, please activate the fast return systems if possible. Nanite suits on."

Hogart pressed a button on his wrist and stayed completely still as his blue nanite suit grew up from his shoes, rushed up the left side of his body, formed a plastic bubble around his head, then grew a mirror version out from the center to envelop his right.

By the time his suit finished forming, Spiney and Cuddly's were already complete.

They all then activated their flash bands and flashed to their designated location, their nanites already working on sterilizing them for the world.

The transition was a bit disconcerting. Hogart had done it many times around the Solar System, but usually not with such a gravity difference. There was usually time to get acclimatized. Even Mars had a way station where you could get used to the gravity before landing on the planet.

He recalled his visit to Mars a few years back. Lots of red, a slightly darker sky, with some blue sky in the morning. The image was quite clear, and the similarities were uncanny.

But this place had some purple and black plants growing in various places, and there seemed to be threads of mist in the air.

His mind-view system told him the threads were small wisps of carbon dioxide. Dry ice. *It must be freezing here.*

He watched some of the mushroom-like bugs in the

distance bouncing along a track towards some conical buildings, then turned to Spiney. "So, they really can't see us?"

"No. Our nanite suits are set to be slightly out of phase with their frequency. We can see them, but they can't see or feel us. The frequency is set for creatures with a higher vibration. The land, rocks and buildings have a lower vibration, so we're able to walk on those, and not fall through the planet."

Suddenly Hogart yelled in surprise. Much to his horror, a large mushroom-bug head started poking out of his stomach, with antennae flicking and twisting. Then the bug creature continued moving with little bounces straight through him. It seemed to be holding some flat things on its underside.

"Oh my God!" Hogart said, slightly shaken, holding his stomach to reassure himself that it was still there.

He was relieved to find that the mushroom-bug had passed completely through him without touching.

Spiney saw his distress. "We best move off the path." He indicated a space where they could get organized, and they headed over to a reddish-tan wall, as more of the bugs bounced past them.

Hogart steadied his breathing then looked closely at the wall. "Industrial printer," he said, indicating the layers of mud. "I guess they're at the equivalent of early 21st century Earth development." He grimaced. "Let's not stay here too long." Then he pointed at the steadily moving groups of mushroom-bugs near them. "They look like they're carrying some kind of material underneath them while they're bouncing. But how are they doing that with no legs? Telekinesis?"

"We're not sure. Perhaps their stomachs are sticky. Lower gravity might mean it is easier to use secretions to retain things."

"Sounds plausible." A useful ability, though he wouldn't like to be stuck to the bottom of one of those things. "Alright," he said. "Cuddly, fill me in. What did Captain Heartness get up to here?"

"Can you see those conical buildings a bit further away?" Cuddly tilted his segmented body towards what looked like a group of reddish-brown dwellings, with three wide entrances positioned equidistant up the side, featuring an adjoining wrap-around ramp. "We had flashed next to one, and thought it was a school. All the young bugs were running in groups to different rooms up the side of the cone, while older bugs looked on. But after Leafy had hijacked the ship and taken us to the other side of the planet, we found evidence of nuclear warfare. So, now we're not sure if it is really a school or not."

"Yes, you can't really tell from here." Hogart was about to rub his chin then remembered he couldn't put his hand through his nanite glass helmet, so changed it to an awkward pointing gesture instead. "Earth wants us to find out whether that is really just a school for general education, or actually a military one. Then we'll decide whether we can instigate first contact."

"Yes," said Spiney. "But if we find out it is a military one, we'll need to add this world to the quarantine list until they are more mature."

"Or begin serious monitoring and intervene if we think this world might become a danger to other worlds," added Cuddly.

"Right, well, let's get on with it."

They set off down the brown and red terrain, walking past and sometimes through many of the mushroom creatures, seeing some having conversations by making a strange scratching sound to get attention, then discussing things with antenna movements.

Many smaller conical buildings dotted the path and Hogart surmised these were living areas, though he couldn't see anything remotely resembling kitchens or toilets. Perhaps the creatures didn't eat.

While watching the creatures on their journey, Hogart thought that he had seen one of them laughing at a joke another had made, giving little jerking movements, but he suspected he was just anthropomorphizing. At this stage he couldn't really tell if there was anything they had in common. If this race was suitable for First Contact, he first had to work out whether they had anything similar to help begin initial conversation or negotiation, but he hadn't found it yet. He'd hate to end up starting with discussing the weather. Especially considering this planet seemed to have a temperate, unchanging climate.

"Cuddly, how is your translator doing?"

Around Cuddly's greenish body, belted between a couple of his sucker feet, was a wide metallic translation system. Unlike the much smaller systems the rest of the crew wore, Cuddly's had a different job. Scanning for, absorbing and interpreting any new languages, and then sending those updates to other crew members.

Cuddly looked down at the flickering lines on its display. "The system estimates it needs another 30,000 sounds before it can begin to construct complicated dialogue. This walk has been very useful, but we're still at larvae level."

"Thank you, Cuddly. Let me know when we're close."

In the lower gravity they made good progress, nanite suits and smooth ground bounding them to the collection of cone buildings in a short time.

Spiney led them to the ramp of the cone Heartness' team had gone to previously, and they set off on the short circular pathway to the top, bypassing the larger base room entrance.

The slope was an easy incline, winding around the cone, with flat landings in front of the doorways. Hogart continued to march upward, then he discovered he was alone and stopped to look back at his slower companions, inching and slapping their way behind him. Perhaps they should have just flashed there directly, but then Cuddly wouldn't have had the chance to absorb the language.

Hogart reached the second room first, and quickly glanced in to see that it was smaller than the base room and with less mushroom-bugs. He guessed that there might be some learning hierarchy with the building. Most would be learning in the bottom room with less and less students able to pass the exams that would enable them to get to the smaller, more advanced rooms nearer to the top.

While he waited for Cuddly and Spiney to catch up, he looked across at the city. Cone-shaped buildings as far as the eye could see with many little brown and black bug shapes scurrying back and forth around them. It was almost like he was in a sophisticated termite town. Or perhaps an advanced ant colony. A few buildings away and to his right was a square with what looked to be an amphitheater, or some kind of meeting place. He activated his mind-view system and zoomed in, but the conical buildings and purple and black leafy plants obscured much of it.

But he was sure there was something gold there. Something that looked out of place compared to the rest of the reddish town. It would be worth checking out.

Spiney and Cuddly reached him, and he continued alongside them, this time attempting to move his legs slow enough to match their inching and slapping.

He had had no idea walking with aliens would be so difficult. Then again, if he was out walking with Puppy, it would be the giant spider-like alien who would be waiting for Hogart.

They reached the third opening, and Spiney stopped outside it. "When the Captain, Leafy and Cuddly returned to the ship without completing the mission, I immediately flashed down to take over. This is the room where I saw markings drawn on the walls that could have been weapons. If there are more here today, I could send these new images back to the team for analysis."

"Lead the way," said Hogart, and they headed inside.

The bright suns and burnished landscape of conical hills outside were in stark contrast to the almost pitch-black interior. Hogart shuddered at the thought of another mushroom-bug walking through him in the dark, and quickly adjusted his light filter.

The room now shone like it was in daylight. Lots of flat rectangular platforms in a semi-circular shape, with many of the mushroom-bugs positioned on them, making scratching noises and flicking their antennae at each other. In the more revealing light, Hogart discovered that they did have eyes, two on each side of the antennae, and two smaller ones just below.

Momentarily distracted by this discovery, he hadn't noticed that Cuddly and Spiney had become silent.

He turned to see that they were staring at whatever had been drawn on the board for the class. Hogart looked over the top of them, then gasped.

He knew it was impossible for that shape to be scratched on that board.

A very familiar shape. A triangle with a sphere in the middle, floating in space.

Then he noticed an arrow-like scratch had been drawn on the board, pointing at it.

"Uh, oh," said Hogart.

Chapter 3
Discovery

Hogart activated his HUD camera and transmitted the disturbing image to the Stellar Flash. "Well, Puppy, what do you think?"

A few seconds later Puppy's translated voice came through from orbit. "We've analyzed the image and can confirm that it is of the Stellar Flash from when we were here last time."

"So, not one of now, then. Perhaps they have a satellite in orbit that we can't detect?"

"Or a powerful telescope," said Geo.

"Good point. But how would they have detected the Stellar Flash? We're supposed to be on another frequency. Completely invisible."

"Leafy had tampered with a variety of systems at the time. I assume our frequency had been detected too," said Amy.

Pilot Leafy had been strongly affected by the binary star system the last time the Stellar Flash had been here. Being a Floran, and having been recently pollinated, she had become mentally unstable, and attempted to release seeds to take over this world.

"Anything else?" Hogart needed to know what to do next. This image changed everything. "What do you think about that scratched line?"

"The arrow could be anything. Distance, planned mission, a missile..."

"Well, I hope it's not the third one." He frowned. This was not a good development. Now that the creatures knew they existed, it was only a matter of time before they worked out where they had come from, and maybe even discover the frequencies of the universes.

He sighed. Not a good start to the mission.

"Okay. Spiney, Cuddly, suggestions, please. They know we exist, but they don't know anything about us. Perhaps we can use this to our advantage. Maybe they really want to meet us?"

"Captain, I'm not sure they're ready," said Cuddly.

"But that's our job. Find out if they're ready, and if they're close, follow the protocols to make them ready. Have you been able to work out their language yet?"

Cuddly indicated his wrap-around translator band. "Almost enough for basic communication. The software should be able to create a sentence soon."

Just then Hogart realized that they had been so focused on discussing the image on the board, they'd forgotten that there were actually mushroom-bug aliens in the room. Hogart turned back to the creatures and stopped, a painful feeling beginning to appear in the pit of his stomach.

Their antennae were all pointing directly at the three crew members. None of them were flicking their antennae at each other. It was like a semicircle of silent spears stabbing towards them, with a slight gap in the middle that led outside.

Had they somehow been detected? Had the mushroom-bugs shifted to the crew's frequency? They still hadn't got the language yet so Hogart didn't want to leave, but perhaps they could run for it and hide out somewhere.

"They're looking at the board, right?" asked Hogart, nervously.

"I don't think so," said Spiney. "This happened to Captain Heartness when her forcesuit was boosted by the EM radiation from the suns. It shifted her frequency slightly closer to theirs and one of them saw her."

"But that's why we're wearing nanite suits!" said Hogart. "Surely they can't pick up on the nanites? Their combined electrical charges are way too small."

Then they both turned to Cuddly, and his whirring, spinning, calculating translator. "It's boosting our bioelectrical signatures!" said Hogart pointing at the device. "It's shifting our frequency closer to theirs! They can *see* us! And you know what that means!"

All three of them turned slowly to look at the mushroom-bugs again. Disturbingly, every single mushroom-bug was one hundred percent focused on the three aliens in front of them.

"What do you think they're going to do?" asked Spiney.

"Three strange creatures suddenly appear in the middle of your classroom? I don't think you're going to offer them a beer!" muttered Hogart.

Then he took a deep breath and without thinking, yelled "Run!" then ran for the doorway, forgetting that Spiney and Cuddly weren't really the running type.

Suddenly, as one, all of the mushroom-bugs leaped forward. There were at least fifteen of the hard brown and black bodies, and now that they'd shifted to their reality, the bugs had no trouble touching them.

Hogart stumbled into the brightness of the blazing

suns and was temporarily blinded as his sensors readjusted to the stronger light. He turned around to make sure his crew were following, then realized that he had forgotten the shapes of his alien crew members. Instantly guilty, he made to go back to save them, but one of the mushroom-bugs was faster, and leaped at him, slamming him to the ground.

He struggled under the creature, the brown and purple sky whirling around him as he desperately tried to shake it off his back.

The creature gripped him as Hogart pulled himself to the edge, looking over the ramp at the ground far below. In this lower gravity, and with the support of the nanite suit, he could probably jump it, but he had no idea what would happen to Spiney and Cuddly. He had to go back and save them.

Using the suit's increased strength-enhancing capabilities, as well as his own power from growing up in the heavier gravity of Earth, he pushed hard against the creature, expecting to throw it against the wall, or at the very least, into the air.

But nothing happened.

Briefly he thought that something had happened to his suit, but he soon realized it was the mushroom-bugs' sticky stomach that had trapped him. He felt a jolt as the creature arched itself slightly, then began bouncing him back through the entrance into the darkened room.

"Lights!" he yelled at his HUD, which quickly showed him the room again.

A reddish blur was spinning near the board and it took him a moment to realize the wild dervish was Spiney, who had worked out a way to stop the creatures from being able to stick to him. He kept spinning fast, his spines knocking a few of the creatures away without hurting them, but they just bounced off the walls and came back at him.

In contrast, Cuddly had just lay down on his side near a corner and curled himself around into a tire shape. He was too soft, even in the nanite suit, and really didn't want to be hurt. He didn't move when a mushroom-bug stuck itself on top of him.

Hogart grunted as the first bug bounced him to the center near the scratch boards, and more of the bugs jumped on top of him. "Come on, guys. You've got me already. No more needed."

With the shaking finally stopping he was able to connect to the ship.

"Stellar Flash, we are under attack," reported Hogart. "You won't be able to activate the fast return switch. The creatures have literally stuck themselves to us, so we can't get a safe relocation signal that takes the suit but not the bug. Stand by."

"I guess it's time to say it then," Spiney's translator stuttered. His spin had been halted by a number of mushroom-bug antenna grabbing him by the spines and lifting him off the ground.

"No. No. I will not say it."

"I will," said Cuddly. "I just finished the translation."

Through the chattering of the bugs, they heard a scratching sound coming from Cuddly. He'd recreated the bugs' speaking alert, and the creatures stopped moving, waiting for the message. Cuddly then sent a signal to his nanite suit to create antennae, similar to the bug on top of him. Five antennae grew out from an area not covered by one of the bugs, made some complicated twisting movements, then stopped.

"Did you say it?" groaned Hogart.

"I said it. Our only option."

"I see," said Spiney.

The mushroom-bugs took a moment to get organized, discussed the issue amongst themselves, made a decision, then curled their bodies slightly to hold Hogart, Spiney and Cuddly in the folds of their stomachs, or whatever they were. Then they began their tiny bounces out of the conical building and down and around the ramp.

Hogart was grateful he wasn't one to get seasick or suffer nausea, and his suit and the lower gravity was protecting him from each landing, but the constant jolting was beginning to give him a pain in the neck, not to mention the constant up and down of the ground affecting his sense of direction. He closed his eyes and waited for them to arrive.

He hoped that they *were* actually taking them to see their leader. If they were just going to throw them in a dungeon and ignore them, he'd have words.

Chapter 4
Contingencies

Admiral Victoria Heartness strode along the cylindrical, carpeted corridor that led to Ring Two.

While Ring Two and Ring Three had spokes and parts of their outer shells already in place, they were nowhere near complete. Engineering had confirmed that, for weight distribution, and artificial gravity alignment, it was better to get all the spokes done first and finalize the ring parts later. For Heartness it was slightly disconcerting to see these almost skeleton-like pieces of the ring just stretching into space, reaching out like reaper's fingers.

She stared out of one of the windows and could see a little EM drone transporting a prefabricate part for the first of the officer's quarters in Ring Two. Perhaps it was carrying the actual wall for her new cabin. For now, she was using the previous Admiral's quarters at the front of the wheel. While ideal when Ring One had first been built, it was now too far away from the action of the rest of the station to be convenient for anyone to find her. Especially on a station this big.

It might be a hundred kilometers long but without any kind of fast tube transport or even fully completed sections, it might as well be a thousand kilometers long.

She shook herself. She was getting maudlin about the end of her starship captain role. She had to keep positive. New position, new job, new challenges. It was going to be great.

With a renewed vigor she looked out another window as she approached the connection to Two. She could see other EM drones flitting about amongst the stars and smiled to herself. There was something comforting about them flying their pieces against the backdrop of Saturn's rings, giving life to the emptiness of space.

Even here, millions of kilometers from Earth, humanity continued to make a home for itself. She idly wondered how many rings would Saturn Base x-1a eventually have? Seven? Ten? Thirty-Four? But things change, and if Earth council suddenly decided it was better to have a station near Pluto, X-1a would become just another tourist destination, like many of the other space stations before it.

The moving walkway in the connecting corridors got her through the main tourism and shopping area, past the station AI's tree avatar, and into the university quarter. She headed to one of the halls on the right where she knew Doctor Hiro Watanabe was giving a remote lecture to the alien students around the base, with a few in physical attendance.

Heartness could not believe she was here. Well, she'd been here many times, but now she was here for a while. A permanent posting next to Saturn for as long as she wanted it. Admiral in charge of Space Station X-1a.

While she'd had her fair share of space station work, and her immediate thought when she'd received her new assignment was *not another space station*, she had been surprised that it was this one.

If it had been one of those positions no one wanted

she would have been disappointed. There were thousands of stations all over the Solar System and they were desperate to get workers in some of them, but X-1a was coveted by most of the space fleet, and for her to get it was the surprise of a lifetime.

She had a feeling she knew why. As this station was going to still be the launching point for the Stellar Flash, if anything went wrong with Hogart's captaincy, she could immediately and easily take over.

Even so, managing a space station wasn't an easy task and so, as she'd had quite a lot of experience managing massive star ships, and was a mean multitasker, she was ideal for the position.

Heartness also suspected she got the job as she had a propensity for making impulsive, instinctual decisions that usually ended up being crucial to survival. With her quirkiness and randomness, if she hadn't got a degree in astrobiology or astrophysics, as well as one as an aeronautical engineer, she suspected she would have ended up as a cat lady on Earth.

Then again, she might still do that.

In the meantime, it was time for one of those impulsive instinctual decisions, and there was only one man that could help her.

She quietly slid through the slightly ajar door of Watanabe's lecture room and stood at the back.

The university room had originally been built to comfortably stand three hundred alien students on several circular steps. Old Earth government officials remembered their grandparents' university days and wanted to spread the traditional style of teaching into space.

Unfortunately, not many modern Earth or alien students were even vaguely interested in standing in a room on a space station for hours when they could simply wait, download the lecture, and fast forward to the good bits. There were also instant upgrade options for those who were compatible. Why spend years studying when you can simply implant the specific work node?

Watanabe ended up being the only one on the whole base using it. In fact, he was probably one of only three lecturers on the station. When teachers could get any teaching node they liked, one teacher could teach thirty different courses a week.

Today he was teaching frequency technology. She knew he liked to hear his voice echo about the chamber, and with their personal cabins quite small, the lecture room gave him the freedom to pace back and forth and wave his arms wide to emphasize a point. Not to mention he loved using magnetic and sense boards, the one behind him now covered in hastily scrawled and almost illegible numbers.

OMG was he really wearing a cardigan? With elbow patches?

She could see him down near the bottom of the room, his white hair askew, his weather beaten and wrinkled face still handsome in his old age, and his one ostentation glittering on one finger, bright even from where Heartness stood – a wedding ring from his late husband.

"And so," Watanabe said with a flourish, his arms flung wide to the empty hall, "what have we learned? We've learned that the universe we live in has a particular beat or pulse that gives it a unique signature. We've also learned that the universe isn't real, it's just a hologram, and it is turned off and on, or destroyed and recreated, every Planck second.

We've learned that in between those beats, when our universe doesn't exist, there are infinite other universes turned off and on at their own different beats, or frequencies. We've learned that, by using the Time and Location vibration mathematics I've described to you today, we can calculate a new TL within another of the universes, apply that TL vibration to anything, and flash it there."

He then noticed Heartness at the back and nodded, then turned to his white board and swiped it, the whiteboard revealing itself to be a solid hologram as it shrank and dissolved back to a crystal projection unit. "Homework will be to calculate your own unique TLV. You can use the quantum computers in hall three to do your calculations. In the next lecture, I will talk about how we create the energy template that enables us to grow the crystalline structure for our flash ships in a bubble reality, and the cycles per second speed required to create the isolation field that enables them to briefly shift outside of one reality and into another. Thank you."

There was a quiet beep, and Watanabe pulled his earpiece out and set it on a nearby table, then strode up the steps to the back of the hall.

"Admiral Heartness," he said, bowing slightly, "What an unexpected pleasure. What brings you here to one of my lectures? You know all this, right? That must have sounded like a massive infodump!" He grinned.

"Doctor Watanabe, it's always good to be refreshed by an expert. You have a certain je ne sai qua when it comes to presenting." Then Heartness became serious. "But, actually, I need your help."

Watanabe bowed again. "At your service, Ma'am."

Heartness looked at him slyly and smiled in a coy way. "You know, Hiro, you don't have to be so formal. And when are we going to get that drink together?"

"Well, I..." Watanabe looked slightly uncomfortable as Heartness moved a little closer. She reached over and adjusted his collar, then, ever so slightly touched his belt, smiling innocently.

"Vicky, you know it hasn't been that long since my husband died. I don't think I'm ready to, you know, try something different. I'm a bit old-fashioned."

"You? You drank all my friends under the table at uni I recall. Even slept with a xeno. And besides, you're still young, not even 69."

"Physically 66. Unofficially, a lot older."

"Oh, soon be middle-aged!"

Watanabe looked at her and laughed. "You've always been after me, as I recall. I'm sorry, but I'm not really like you modern people. I'm a one-man guy."

"Well, you know where to find me if you ever change your mind."

Watanabe smiled. "Of course. Now, Vicky darling, what can I do for you?"

Heartness straightened her top and tried to act official. It was difficult with her long-term friend. She loved him dearly, and would most definitely have liked to have been able to love him in other ways, but she'd been in the friend-zone for years. Still, she loved just sitting, drinking and chatting with him and didn't want to lose that. She turned back to the task at hand. "I need you to grow me an interfrequency scout ship, asap."

Watanabe looked at her and raised an eyebrow.

"Hmm. I guess it's a need to know, and I don't need to know?"

Heartness nodded.

"Very well," Watanabe sighed. Then he thought for a moment and his face widened into a beaming smile. "My next lecture is on growing flash ships. No one has created a lecture while they're actually growing one. My ratings would go through the roof!"

"Just don't say what it is for or install the cockpit controls on camera. Make it look like you just set it up for the lecture, then didn't finish it."

"Of course. Is this for you personally?"

"Yes."

"Then I'll set up a frequency resonance similar to your brainwaves so you can pilot it. I will have it ready within about two hours."

"Hangar 16?"

"I believe so. If anything changes, I'll let you know."

"Thank you, Hiro. I'll see you there."

This time they both gave each other a hug, and Heartness left him to close up, striding back down the corridor to her wheel section.

It wouldn't do for her to only be able to travel between here and Earth. Especially with no flash ships scheduled to appear anytime soon.

It really didn't take them that long to make flash ships. They just cost a lot. Multiple teams of skill contributors would need to generate thousands of exchange hours of labor before they could trade for the materials. She knew Watanabe would use some of their repair crystal supplies to create a small one, but it would take the satellite months before the satellite could acquire more.

She just hoped it would be worth it.

She smiled ruefully to herself. Just a few days after completing her final mission and she was already getting cabin fever.

But, her years in the other frequencies had given her a stronger feeling about possible futures. And her intuition was now telling her that the crew of the Stellar Flash might need her, and that trouble was on the horizon.

A lot of trouble.

Chapter 5
Take Me to Your Leader

The gold mushroom-bug was at least ten meters wide. It sat on a large red rectangular podium in a space similar to a town square. It was surrounded by groups of smaller black and brown bugs that kept spitting on it. Well, Hogart thought it was spit. Some kind of chemical that spurted from the base of the antennae. They were either trying to keep the Queen cool, or this was the way the mushroom-bug ate. He decided not to think too much about the second possibility.

Perhaps this was the gold thing he saw before.

The bugs had released them, leaving their nanite suits covered in a sticky slime, and now they stood waiting while Cuddly flicked his antennae around.

"Cuddly, is this their leader?"

Cuddly spun and began flicking his antennae at Hogart. His translator translated. "Yes. This is Queen Unpronounceable, the leader of this planet. She had detected our presence and changed the frequency of her bioelectrical signals to enable us to meet her."

She can do that? Hogart thought, concern suddenly filling him. So, it wasn't the translator that had given them away. The Queen had some skills of her own.

Then a further thought worried him. If she could detect their original frequency, she might even be able to transport herself to Saturn.

Then he chided himself. Their capture could just be

the way they treat visitors here. He shouldn't assume the worst. He should be more positive at a time like this. This could be official First Contact. He had to follow protocol.

"Please tell her we are honored to meet her and would like her to know about alien life, and whether she feels her world would be ready for a first contact situation, or even an exchange in technology."

More waving of antennae, and Cuddly's translator had trouble getting the English words out.

"She doesn't know what you mean. She has never met anything that wasn't part of her System before. This is a confusing situation."

"She doesn't travel?"

"No, captain. System as in the population system. All the mushroom-bugs are different parts of her."

Hogart thought about this for a moment. Was it like an ant or aphid colony? Or were they more like molds?

"Telepathically linked? Hive mind? Clones? Amoebas?"

"Actually, they're like you." replied Cuddly. "You're an individual but you have a symbiotic relationship with billions of different types of bacteria that live in specific areas of your body. The bacteria are yours, are part of you, but they can leave and go elsewhere if they wish."

"These darker bugs are like her bacteria? But connected to her?" asked Spiney. "So, there is only really one alien ready for first contact, and we have just done that!"

Hogart looked at the giant creature carefully. It was at least three times the size of the largest mushroom-bug they'd met, and seemed to have two sets of antennae, one on each side of it. Only one set seemed to be working, but, apart from that, the body almost seemed to be a mirror image on both sides. Like two insects joined together at the base.

"I don't think she is the only one," he said.

"Captain!" said Spiney. "You cannot simply disagree when we are at the beginning of a relationship. You need to see the other side!"

"I am seeing the other side. Both of her sides! She says she doesn't know any 'other' but your previous trip discovered evidence of a nuclear war, and now she's about to split into two creatures. She's like an amoeba. How many times do you think she's gone through mitosis? They may be part of her from her perspective, but I think they're a lot more individual than that."

Hogart was thinking about the school. *If you're really all the same, why do you need a school?*

"What about the others of your race?" asked Cuddly, taking everything Hogart had just said, and combining it into a much shorter sentence for the translator.

The Queen shifted on her hill, and a flash of gas puffed out from between her, just as her body lengthened further. Was she going to split now?

"Gone," said the translator. "Other places. Create their own systems. Come back to take ours."

"You've been fighting yourself?" asked Hogart. "Or your children?"

"Activating automatic," said Cuddly. "The system can translate between you and her now."

The Queen flicked her antennae and Cuddly's translator answered. "Must have technology. Must leave this world. Start again."

Hogart looked at Spiney and Cuddly. Then he turned to the Queen and said, "I'm really sorry Queen, but we cannot help you in this way. We can only give you technology to help your world. It is up to you to develop off world technology at this time."

The Queen's antennae on the other side of her body suddenly started moving.

"Unacceptable. You will be dismembered," Cuddly translated, shaking.

"Dismembered? Well," said Hogart, "I'm not ready for the higher frequencies just yet. Okay team, activate your flash bands. Let's get out of here. Cuddly, don't translate that."

Cuddly's antennae moved. "I'm sorry, captain. The translator is on automatic."

Hogart suddenly found that, even though he was free of the mushroom-bugs, they'd actually glued his feet to the ground. He realized that the others were equally stuck, glued to their positions. Perhaps he could program his flash band to take the glue with him?

Then he noticed the Queen's antennae had started moving, and the mushroom-bugs jumped them again. As soon as the bugs stuck to him, Hogart knew he wasn't going anywhere.

"Sir," interrupted Spiney. "I think we should go through the correct channels and follow the rules of queen unpronounceable. After all, we are a guest on her world."

"Queens," corrected Cuddly.

"Queens? Already?" asked Hogart.

There was another blast of gas, a large scraping sound, and suddenly the gold queen completely separated in the middle. The ends with antennae on the left and right turned to face the crew, both antennae going wild.

"Captain," said Cuddly, "I can't manage two queens at once!"

"Count yourself lucky. Some men never get the chance," muttered Hogart, as several more mushroom-bugs bounced towards them.

"We have got the sound, thanks to Cuddly. Now for the picture." Geo placed one of his drops against his white surface display and zoomed the Center's surround screen down to the planet. The rest of the crew watched as the images shifted from the suns to the planet then focused on a section of the city and continued to enlarge. The AI compensated for orbital drift, and the image stabilized.

From above they could see the mushroom-bugs bouncing Hogart, Spiney and Cuddly down a pathway, with two huge yellow ones sitting on a raised area, their antennae moving frantically at each other.

"That doesn't look good," said Puppy.

"Can you translate?" asked Geo.

"Working on it," said Amy. "Cuddly has transmitted the translation update, but it's incomplete. He's still analyzing the language. It might not be clear enough."

Two voices came through the intercom.

"I want dismembered them."

"No, their current shapes might use."

"I take ship leave."

"You first need there get. You just born. Know not anything."

"I enough. Your memories. Ice volcano, escape velocity, telekinetic guidance. Match velocity, land on ship."

"We negotiate. Technology for other planets. They help."

Puppy paused the image. "Both sides of herself fighting over the crew members. I'm betting on the 'mother.'

"It is possible that the more mature alien will prevail in this discussion," said Torus. "But the younger one may just kill her and take over, or perhaps order other parts of herself to kill the crew. We need to work something out."

"Team," began Amy. "I'm not sure that the mushroom-bugs are from here. Their chemistry seems to be more advanced than the planet they're on."

Torus and Puppy were silent as they digested this piece of information.

"Invaders or panspermia?" asked Geo.

"I suspect both, based on what Queen Two just said. If they use volcanoes to launch themselves across space to other low gravity planets, who knows how many they occupy."

"So, it's possible that, if there was a more primitive group of mushroom-bugs on this world already, this group nuked them and took over," said Puppy. "They may have taken over other worlds."

"But," said Geo. "This system contains thirty planets of different sizes. Do you think they have survived landing on all of them?"

"We don't know for sure, but after we rescue our surface team, we're going to have to investigate all the other planets."

"That could take months!"

Puppy thought for a moment, then spoke to the air.

"AI, do we have enough information to create drones that can operate and report back in this frequency?"

"Yes, Officer Puppy."

"Very good. Activate our robot construction bay and begin production. You will oversee the process."

"Confirmed."

On one of the edges of the Stellar Flash, lit by the brown and purple planet, a light began flickering. Inside the window, several robot arms began extending from the walls and pulling pieces together on a circular table. Nozzles and tubes fell from the ceiling, wires and other items sprung from the floor, and a welder began connecting parts.

The AI's Japanese form looked seriously over the construction. She was interfaced with the ship and knew all the systems, but sometimes she enjoyed using her external hologram just for the different perspective it gave.

Sparks and beams of light played through her image as further metal pieces began coming together in front of her - spheres about the size of a human fist, equipped with flash technology. As the final piece of each drone was inserted, it activated, glowed, then flashed and disappeared.

Closer to the two stars, a blueish brown planet spun slowly. A flash appeared in the atmosphere, and a drone materialized in a low orbit, quickly flitting amongst the threads of clouds, heading towards the surface.

The AI watched as another drone flashed and disappeared.

This one appeared near a smaller, almost dark brown world, with the binary stars very small in the background. The drone engaged its EM thrusters to investigate, heading for the planet.

Another drone disappeared from the AI's factory on the Stellar Flash. Another signal was reported back to her. She displayed it on the analysis screen in the foundry as other signals began coming in, sent instantly via quantum entanglement, rather than the hours a normal signal might take to reach the ship.

As the messages flashed on the screen, she calculated that Captain Hogart may not be happy with this result.

>LIFE DETECTED
>LIFE DETECTED
>LIFE DETECTED
>LIFE DETECTED
>LIFE DETECTED

Chapter 6
Stuck

Hogart strained again at the sticky glue that held him in place against the smooth red wall. They had been bounced to a room inside one of the nearby conical buildings, unceremoniously thrown in, then glued down wherever they landed.

The room was about eight meters square with flat walls, but it didn't really look like a cell. Hogart guessed the planet rarely had a use for a cell, if all the aliens were part of one creature.

The small entrance had been big enough to push them inside, but that was now filled in by a combination of rocks and glue. Even if the room had had an Earth atmosphere, the blocked door and smooth walls and ceiling meant they would have all suffocated within the hour.

Hogart strained against the glue again, but had already decided that, unless he dissolved his nanite suit, he had no way of getting out of this. And with no air nearby that he could breath, that would mean instant death.

Then Hogart saw that Cuddly was inching back and forth. He wasn't stuck! Cuddly could click on his flash band at any time.

"Cuddly, get out of here. You don't need to stay with us."

"I'm still absorbing their language. You need a

communications officer. I can't leave you here."

Hogart was quietly grateful that Cuddly didn't want to leave, and he really did need a communications officer. But then he noticed that he was moving erratically around the room, his body showing signs of distress.

"I appreciate that very much Cuddly, but you look like you're not happy about something. Why are you walking back and forth like that?"

"I have to go, captain," said Cuddly, with a slight panic to his voice.

"But, you just said you wanted to stay."

"No, I need to, you know, go."

Cuddly looked about, wondering why the captain wasn't quite understanding him. Then he understood.

"Apologies Captain. Translator is highly euphemistic. Software, give direct translation for 'need to go.'"

The band around Cuddly's body flickered for a moment, then said "Ablutions."

"Oh. Well. You should just do it in the corner," said Hogart, dismissively.

"But..."

"We're all adults here, Cuddly. "We won't be embarrassed."

"Captain," interrupted Spiney from his sideways position on the floor. "I think what Cuddly is trying to say is that, as his waste is highly toxic, we might be affected by it."

"Really? In our suits?"

"Captain," implored Cuddly. "It might cause your nanite suits to malfunction."

"One of my colleagues was like that. Sometimes we couldn't go into the restroom for days." Hogart did his best to say it with a straight face.

"Did he blow up a wall?"

Hogart's mouth open and closed again. *Seriously?* "Cuddly, I didn't study your genotype, but if you're able to release something so highly dangerous, how is it you're able to actually keep it in your body in the first place?" Hogart looked incredulously at him.

"Dual bladders," said Spiney. "When the chemicals mix they can cause some damage, even dissolve rock. Cuddly's race evolved this method of defense."

"Can it dissolve through glue?"

The aliens were silent.

"Well?" asked Hogart.

Cuddly came over slowly, almost like he was admitting some terrible secret. "I can dissolve anything."

"Wow, Cuddly. That's incredible. Why haven't you used this skill before?"

"Skill?"

"Come on ma... err officer, you should be positive about this. We can't carry guns unless we're on the offensive. You've basically got a secret weapon! Unlike Spiney here whose weapons are pretty obvious, and my fists have way too many other functions. You're a walking bomb!"

"Err. Thanks. I think."

"Start with Spiney."

"What? Captain, I object," said Spiney.

"He just needs to spray a bit around your edges, and it'll dissolve the glue, then you can get up."

"It'll dissolve my nanite suit. My spines are more like fingers than spikes. I'll feel every drop!"

"He'll be careful, won't you Cuddly?"

"Um, I'm not sure I can aim straight enough," said

Cuddly, apologetically.

Hogart rolled his eyes. *Aliens!* "I don't even know why I'm discussing this with you. Cuddly, I order you to piss on Spiney."

"Captain!"

"Spiney, get back to the ship using any means necessary. Once you're there, you can mount a rescue attempt, if they haven't already organized one." Hogart struggled against the glue on the wall, but there still wasn't any give. He would have to stay. "I'm hoping, err, I don't think Cuddly can't spray this high."

Cuddly stood there, rocking back and forth, unsure, embarrassed, and no doubt wondering what kind of report he would get after urinating on a superior officer. "I'm really sorry, Spiney."

"Just do it," said Spiney, resigned.

Cuddly rose his front, and Hogart was surprised to see that the two, middle sucker-like legs were extending, and the suit nanites were making holes in the front, ready to release their loads. He now knew he would be looking at Cuddly's private parts every day and had already been doing that without even knowing it.

Hogart closed his eyes and shook his head. Too much information. He'll make sure he never notes this when he returns to Frequency Zero. Or, at the very least, avoid reading Jorjarar's report of it.

Just as Cuddly was about to begin, there was a scratching sound, and the dramatic thump thump thump of several mushroom-bugs pounding towards them.

Surprised at the sudden noise, Cuddly straightened up quickly, and involuntarily emptied both his bladders at the filled-in doorway. As soon as both liquid streams hit the rocks and glue, there was a minor explosion and it collapsed, burying bugs and blocking their escape.

Cuddly shook from the reaction, then slowly inched back and curled up on the floor, the shame and embarrassment making him speechless.

Hogart looked at the mess, the struggling mushroom-bugs, and the curled-up form of Cuddly. Not only were they trapped, they might have just started a war.

"Well done, Cuddly," Hogart sighed.

He wondered if Heartness had ever been in this situation. If she had, he'd definitely like to know how she had been able to get out of it.

Chapter 7
Breach

The six smaller domes surrounding the larger central dome creaked and shifted in the icy winds that streamed along the snow-covered mountains. The Enceladus base on one of Saturn's moons was a new outpost, created by another of Earth's research and development departments. Cratered ice stretched as far as the eye could see, rarely broken by the tracks of the landers.

Not far from the base, a force dome flickered, standing out starkly against the white environment. A lone suited figure peered cautiously through the energy barrier at a turquoise bulge of ice that poked through the otherwise featureless surface.

Doctor John Patel shivered in his space suit. Even though he was enjoying the twenty-four-degree warmth and slight humidity of his enclosed environment, what was under that ice bulge was not something he really wanted to be next to. Even with his decades of training and experience, and multiple knowledge upgrades, he still wasn't entirely comfortable with unknown dangers in a darkened enclosed space.

He'd recently taken up spelunking on the various moons around Saturn, and had the experience needed for investigating air pockets under the surface. Though, when he was called in to investigate this one, he quickly learnt that it was a lot more than just an air pocket.

He scrolled for the address link and pressed the relocation button on his suit, rematerializing a few meters down. A dark, bubble-shaped space - he couldn't believe that yesterday there had been no evidence of its existence. Just a few hours ago, all the base's sensors had gone wild, detecting the vibration of this thing that had appeared out of nowhere.

As soon as he adjusted to the little light filtering through the solid ice above, he began broadcasting to X1-a. There would be a few seconds delay before the Admiral received his message, so he began his report without waiting for a reply.

Admiral Victoria Heartness looked at the image in shock. Patel had been playing xenoarchaelogist, and he'd just started streaming a creature stuck half in the ice and half in the rock. The creature was frozen solid and looked like it had been there for a very long time.

But it was unmistakable. A mushroom-bug. A small, gold-colored one.

She connected, and immediately spoke. She knew it would be a few seconds before he got the message, and there was no point in wasting time with hellos and how are yous.

"How did it get there, Patel?"

On Heartness' monitor the space-suited scientist-cum-secret services operative shrugged in the shadowed environment, his helmet light reflecting the creature in disturbing gold flickers. "I'm detecting a phase shift. It looks like it arrived out of phase with the matter around it, and quickly tried to change frequency. I've never seen a creature with rock actually interspersed throughout it before. It usually replaces it, not merges with it. It's definitely not fossilized."

"Is there any chance it can phase out again? Is it dormant or dead?" She was getting a sinking feeling about this. How could the creature have crossed the frequencies? More importantly, how could they have crossed to this particular frequency? There were billions to choose from.

"I really couldn't say, admiral. But there's one more thing. I'm detecting negative time around it. According to the surrounding rock and ice, it's probably been here for thousands of years, but the system is saying that it doesn't exist yet. In fact, negative time will reach zero in about ten minutes. So, it's like it is in a holding pattern in time, waiting for time to catch up to it."

Heartness sat back in her chair and stared at the screen. If the mushroom-bugs had suddenly found a way to get to their solar system without permission, then they were no longer a potential first contact species, they were a threat.

"Patel, get a contingent of guards down there. I want guns. I want forcefields. I want that entire area cordoned off. Get the Enceladus AI to run a scan around the nearby ice for any more mushroom bugs that may have made it through. I'd hate to think there was an army hiding in the ice. If these creatures start spreading here, who knows what damage they can do to the Solar System."

"Yes, ma'am. Understood."

Heartness disconnected and pondered the situation. In a few minute's time, that mushroom-bug would officially arrive. Was it a coincidence, or was it something that Hogart had caused? She needed more information, but she didn't have any Flash ships she could call upon. Of course, Watanabe was already growing her a small one. Her intuition had been right. But she needed more before she chased after the Stellar Flash.

But there was also Earth. Was this a foothold situation? She could send a quantum entangled signal to Earth for emergency help, but what if there were mushroom bugs monitoring communications? They'd be giving their position away.

She'd only been in the role of admiral, and responsible for thousands of people on X-1a, for just a few hours, and already she was facing the possibility of a mass invasion of the Solar System from another frequency.

She wondered if previous admirals had had similar situations, and they were simply forgotten or covered up in the rush for the stars.

Well, she'd better make sure her first one was not her last.

She switched on the announcement system. "This is Admiral Victoria Heartness. A potential threat has been discovered on Enceladus. As a safety precaution, all transmissions to Earth will be suspended as of this moment. If there is some other absolute emergency that may cause a problem for everyone on the base, and require Earth reinforcements, come to my office directly to talk with me about it. All tourism and deliveries will be suspended until further notice. All scheduled delivery ships will be reflashed to Titan base until the emergency is over. I apologize for any inconvenience yada yada."

She ended the transmission and sat back in her

chair. It would be just over an hour before Earth knew they'd been cut off, sooner if someone tried to flash jump.

She only hoped Hogart knew what he was doing. If he was the cause of the mushroom-bug arriving in a few minutes time, she'd have words with him.

If they survived it.

Patel made to run his hands through his hair but remembered he was wearing his old chunky space suit and stopped. He couldn't even rub his chin, or stroke his white, toothbrush moustache, and the puffy suit weighed down on him. Even though the bubble of air in the cavern was hydrogen and oxygen, without a carbon dioxide scrubber, he wouldn't be able to live long if he took his helmet off.

He shivered, irrationally wondering if another mushroom-bug was about to make an appearance behind him.

The creature in front of him didn't look that close to the sketches drawn by the crew members from the previous mission to the mushroom-bugs' world.

There was no record of any color other than browny-purply-black, and they weren't drawn like this. He wished he could have gotten better images, but they hadn't thought to send artists on that particular mission. And, even then, they may not have been able to recreate it exactly when they got back.

Shifting frequencies not only messed with people's minds, it also translated the images they remembered differently. He'd never been to Frequency One, but he understood it was like seeing a tesseract there, a six 'cube'-sided cube, and then trying to take the image back to Frequency Zero and draw it. The human mind would end up with a six 'square'-sided cube. Sometimes it wasn't possible to bring back the correct image of something.

But he did know that if the original item from that frequency somehow made it into this, then it would transform to match the memories of how those in Frequency Zero now perceived it.

This gold mushroom-bug had never been seen before by anyone in this universe.

He walked back and forth in front of the ice wall, looking at the alien's warped image, the helmet light breaking up its reflection in the hard wall. Five antennae at the front with plating across its oval back that was made up of millions of tiny pieces. The alien looked like a trilobite-shaped mushroom with feelers.

He couldn't see its underside, but he suspected that it might have something concealed there. Was it part of it, or was it holding something?

He leant against the wall and pondered the creature, checking the time. Five minutes until time reached zero. Would the creature suddenly become active? And would the resulting time bubble affect him? He'd been able to flash here with no problems, so assumed he wasn't part of the bubble. But there was always the chance of some kind of external effect.

He turned on his recording equipment. "Analysis suggests the creature has flashed across the frequencies. It's possible it has used some kind of remote jumping technology, but without any way of returning, it would be a suicide mission. I suspect that the device is with it and we just can't see it."

He was thankful the admiral hadn't blocked his messages, and he was able to get a request to the space station's AI to do a complete scan from above and below. He'll investigate the records of the creature when he got back.

He looked around the small cavern, careful not to move too fast in the low gravity. He didn't want to bounce into the ice wall. "How'd you get here, Blondie?" he said aloud. "Are you working with someone?"

He held the data pad in front of him, speaking for his report, filling in time before the security guards arrived.

Something flickered out of the corner of his eye. He turned and saw a rivulet of water and stared at it in surprise.

"What?"

It took him a moment to realize what was happening. His HUD said the external temperature was minus one hundred and ninety-two degrees Celsius. Running water couldn't exist.

He shone his light along the glassy ice. More rivulets.

But there was something else strange about them. They just didn't look right. If he could have taken his helmet off and had a closer look...

Just then, five security personnel flashed in.

"Doctor Patel, my team and I are here to watch the creature. You can leave it to us." The guard brandished what looked to be some kind of plasma bazooka. "If it wakes up, we'll take care of it."

Patel knew not to bother trying to explain the whole reverse-time effect, but he had to turn back to the water. It was completely impossible. "Just one moment. I don't know why water is running here. It's too cold for it. I need to check..."

He took a closer look and stepped back. The water

was running backwards. *Up* the wall of ice.

Patel opened his mouth and closed it again. He should have guessed. The creature's phasing was about to happen, but it was happening in reverse. From its perspective, it had already died through being frozen - forward in time for it. But for Patel and the team, everything was backward for them. That meant that its appearance must have vaporized the ice, which then melted and froze quickly.

Then Patel swore, and almost smashed his gloved hand against his helmet in realization.

That was the reason there was an atmosphere in here in the first place. The creature's appearance had created it. And if it leaves, the pocket would be instantly filled with ice.

"Emergency evacuation!" yelled Patel. "It's about to implode. Get out. Press your addresses. Return to the base!"

The security personnel knew not to argue, and immediately tapped their wrists and disappeared. Patel glanced around furtively. Had he left anything? No.

He watched as more rivulets of water sprung from the ground and began streaming towards the block of ice above – a torrential up-pour.

The wall of water started moving inexorably towards him, like some ancient ocean demon out for revenge.

He quickly slapped his address button, closed his eyes, gritted his teeth and flashed back to the surface.

Just as Patel vanished, the creature disappeared, and the cavern was instantly filled with ice that had been there for eons, like nothing had ever happened.

Patel was back at the base; his suit helmet off. He'd got back to his temporary quarters and activated the contact screen while unclipping his gloves and boots.

"Please leave a message," said the AI.

Patel sighed. Heartness insisted on her breaks.

"Well, I'm sure you're taking some time off, Admiral, so I'll be brief. I don't think you'll like what I found. I'll send the details encrypted to the X-1a's AI. Your authorization only."

He flicked a switch, then swiped the information from his tablet to the screen in front of him.

"Attachments sent," said the AI.

He'd seen the scans made by X-1a and knew that Hogart was to blame. He would have to have a chat with him when he got back. Not just because what he had done was against the laws of the Earth government, but because it was impossible. He not only wanted to know why, he wanted to know how.

If Hogart made it back.

Admiral Heartness was enjoying a brief respite from the stuffiness of her cabin, taking a walk through the center of the space station. If the mushroom-bugs were going to invade, she had to be clear-minded and relaxed, and what better way to relax than to have a closer look at the AI's artwork-avatar.

Passing several alien tourist stores that were promoting amazing collections of items from around the galaxy, she headed for what looked like a large plant-root system that spread out along the adjoining corridors and across various connecting bridges. A massive trunk spread upwards, branching into, well, branches that impossibly pierced the glass canopy into the vacuum, and seemed to wave slowly at the nearby rings of Saturn.

Space Station X-1a's AI's image this week was a tree, representing the silky oaks of Australia. A thick body with rough bark that seemed to surround it in thousands of soft sticks, the tree filled the central restaurant promenade of Ring One, its branches each ending in a small AI access terminal where tourists could ask questions or check messages.

Tourists gawked and snapped images around her, while personnel took their drinks or food to check status updates.

Heartness smiled to herself at all the happy people, then walked to the lift vestibule. Hopefully, she'd be able to lift the travel ban soon, and everyone could get on with their lives. Thankfully, no one yet knew what she looked like, so most tourists thought she was just another personnel member. Even if they had noticed her stripes, they wouldn't know what they meant.

She checked her flash band. A message from Patel with an attachment. She couldn't check it so close to so many people. If the news was bad, it would spread like wildfire, and make controlling everyone so much harder. She decided to access the files from one of the less-used terminal areas near the top.

The lift only took a minute to get there, and she was pleased to find no one was up this high. With no shops, and only another window showing the rings, it wasn't the most popular area. She liked to come here on her breaks, sit by herself and watch the crowds below.

Of course, she could have gone back to her office to check Patel's files, but she had those kilos to work off. She didn't want to end up with seat-butt.

"Voice authorization Heartness One. AI open the attachments recently sent by Doctor John Patel."

"Yes, Admiral."

The AI opened the files as a hologram in front of her. A rough frequency scan and animated reconstruction of the frozen mushroom-bug up to the point it disappeared.

The main recording had been made from above, and she watched as Patel stepped backwards, madly hit his arm to disappear as a wall of water came closer to him, then the creature's antennae had begun to move as the ice melted around it.

Then it had simply disappeared, and solid snow had filled the pocket.

"AI, reverse playback."

She watched as there was a flash, the snow exploded into a bubble, and the creature materialized, half in ice and half in rock, then it twitched a few times and was still, as Patel came closer.

"AI, confirm that this was a flash band entry."

"Yes, Admiral. Isolation field matrix is indicative of Earth technology."

Heartness knew the only real way the creature could have materialized is if it had somehow got hold of a flash band. The flash bands were programmed with all the Solar System's bases' locations in space/time, and automatically calculated the exact vibration to be able to change the location coordinates of the traveler. But they weren't designed for mushroom-bugs, which was probably why the creature had materialized inside rock.

"AI, show me the underside of the creature."

Heartness hoped her hunch wasn't right, but as the AI shifted to the other composite image, a frequency scan that had been conducted through the south pole of the moon to the bottom of the creature, she could see the evidence underneath. A bright silver flash band concealing almost all of the alien's underside.

And not just any old flash band.

It was Hogart's.

Heartness looked at it with sadness. "Oh, Jonathan. What have you done?"

Chapter 8
A Gift in Time

Now that three of the crew were in danger, Puppy was in charge. He stood on his twelve stick-like legs near one of the three entrances to the Center, towering over everything, and overseeing the progress.

The crew knew the humans would not be happy to find that the star system was teeming with life. If what the Queen said was true, life on the other planets would most likely be more queens and their bacteria.

The drones were still on the way to the surface of the other worlds in the star system, so they hoped to get more comprehensive results within the hour. But if all the planets contained these mushroom-bugs, then it might be a huge risk asking them to join the IC.

Then again, the humans had spread across the planets of their Solar System before their Shift had happened, and they had been fairly well-behaved after joining.

"AI, please take my report," said Puppy.

The AI's Japanese avatar immediately appeared, and Puppy looked her up and down. "Why does Hogart like this form? Is it pleasing for him?"

"On some parts of planet Earth, this form is attractive. Hogart just likes looking at what he considers to be pretty faces. He'll be away from humans for a while, so something familiar will help him cope mentally. If you miss your race, I can be someone for you, too!"

"I guess beauty is in the eye of the beholder," said Puppy, wagging his body a little. "Well, there's nothing more I can do for the moment, so I've got a bit of time. Okay, change for me."

The AI immediately changed into another alien like Puppy but with ten legs, a smaller tongue and bigger mandibles.

"Oh, hellooo," said Puppy. "Even up-to-date with the ten-leg trend. And the drool... How sexy are you! You look barely out of your egg!"

The six-eyed, ten-legged spider-like alien seemed to shuffle a bit in what humans might have considered coyness.

"Now, that's a pretty face! Thank you, AI. This form is much better. Let's have you like that for now." Then Puppy turned to the center of the Center. "Okay, team. Time for an English report for the human race. Are we ready?"

"Aye, aye captain," said Amy's translator. She was the only one there.

"Officer Puppy reporting for the humans. Captain Jonathan Hogart, First Officer Spiney and Communications Officer Cuddly have been captured by mushroom-bugs on Planet Brown and Purple. Monitored communications suggest that Queen Unpronounceable has split into two queens and that there is a chance they will kill our crew members if we don't give them flash technology."

"Right so far, though I think she said dismember," said Amy.

"'Dismember' it is. We assume that this has not yet

happened as we expect some kind of ultimatum or hostage negotiation to take place. However, we have not been able to contact the crew since they were taken inside one of the conical buildings, and assume that they have chosen communications silence for security."

"Correct."

"Drones have been sent by the AI to thirty planets in the star system, with about ten so far confirmed by quantum entanglement to have life. We suspect that this life is the same form as below but are waiting more detailed reports. We should know for sure within the hour. If these creatures have spread throughout the star system, and are fighting amongst each other, then the quarantine protocol must be enacted until they have evolved further."

"Yes," said Amy.

"We have decided that more detailed investigations are required, in order to analyze the exact chemical the mushroom creatures are secreting, so that we can rescue the crew members from their prison. To this end Officer Geo and Officer Torus, along with a small contingent of security personnel, have arrived in an area on the night side to capture one of the aliens. Incidentally, I have decided to name the aliens, for easy news reports for Earth, Mushbugs."

"Mushbugs?" asked Amy. "Why didn't you ask me? I'm an astrobiologist! They should be called Eukaryotoid Amoeboid Protists! They're not at all related to mushrooms or fungi or bugs! Why not EAPs?"

"Thank you, Amy. Mushbugs it is."

If Amy had been human, she probably would have rolled her eyes.

"Here ends the report," said Puppy.

The AI bent on her pole-like legs and straightened again. "Shall I get back to my duties?" she burbled.

"What, you don't want to just stand there and look sexy for me? Love what you've done with your back hair. Oooh, and you've got mandible extension! Mmm Mmm"

"I think this form is too much of a distraction for you, Officer Puppy."

Puppy clacked his front legs together and gave a sound almost like sighing. "Alright, if you insist. Amy?"

"All you aliens are so specific in what you like. I must say, I don't really understand. If it's got holes, I'm in."

"Sorry?"

"I love merging with another being and just travelling in and out of all their holes. Especially their pores. Getting deep into an entity from every angle. That's the most amazing feeling. Do you know humans actually have seven holes in their head, and they're all connected? I can slide through their skulls! But it's not just humans. Look at you. Are those legs hollow?" Amy's gelatinous body twisted and turned, reaching out a translucent tentacle to touch one of Puppy's legs.

Puppy, immediately concerned, stepped back a little. "Amy, we've been on missions before and you never said anything about being, you know, xenocurious with me. What's got into you?"

Amy flickered, changing color a few times, settled on green, then turned back to her computer, a bit distracted. "Anyway, I can do that with anything. Even this computer. But you're right, Puppy. I'm definitely feeling more amorous than usual. It must be the binary stars." Amy looked at the image of the AI. "Can you give me a piece of pumice from Earth?"

The AI's hairy, ten-legged alien disappeared and was replaced with a darkish grey rock with millions of tiny little holes in it. Amy almost collapsed into a puddle at the sight.

"Oh, even more beautiful than I remember. When I discovered these volcanic rocks on Earth, I locked myself in my cabin for days. Amazing experience. Not very conversational, though."

"You're joking!"

"I think this is a better choice for an image, don't you think?"

"A rock!"

"The AI can speak through something else, and she doesn't need an image anyway. It's just for us to have a direction to speak towards."

Puppy clacked his legs. Perhaps it was best not to be too distracted. In any case he was looking forward to seeing Hogart's reaction when they got him back. "You're right, Amy. AI, I hope you're alright with being a rock for a while."

"Yes, Officer Puppy, Officer Amy. I am very happy to be a piece of pumice stone."

Just then the rock began flashing red. "Results are in," said the AI.

"And?" asked Amy.

"Confirmed. All thirty planets, several moons and even a few asteroids and comets contain mushbugs. And they're all fighting each other for resources."

"It's an infestation. We can't let them know about Earth," said Amy. "Or our entire universe, for that matter."

"We may need to quarantine the entire star system," said Puppy.

"Additional," interrupted the AI. "Cyborg bacteria detected on most of the outward planets, capable of adding huge concentrations of carbon dioxide to the atmosphere."

Amy quickly splashed herself across her console. "Analysis confirms that is how the mushbugs have been able to spread. The first one brings the bacteria. The second arrives on a world ready for it. If even a few of these bacteria make it onto our ship, they'll change our air, and all the oxygen breathing crew will die. Not only that, but bacteria can sometimes cross between frequencies. They'll get back to the Solar System and begin converting everything. We can't let them get on board."

"But that's the outer planets. What about this one? Any sign?"

"Checking. Analysis confirms. Not as virulent but there are strains on the planet below."

"And we've just sent Geo and Torus to capture a bacteria-covered mushbug," said Puppy.

Geo and Torus looked on while five of the security personnel began herding a mushroom-bug towards them. The personnel were chosen purely because they had arms and legs ideal for capturing something - appendages that both Geo and Torus lacked.

"I never thought we'd be out trying to catch something," said Geo, as a six-armed bear-like alien in a nanite suit held its arms out towards the creature. The mushroom-bug turned each way, trying to find a way to get through, but the five personnel came closer, circling it. "I'm a first contact specialist, not a zookeeper."

"I do prefer utilizing the phase-shifting magnet. It is much more professional. But with these creatures finding a way to appear to us in this frequency, there is a risk of them shifting out of it." Torus held up the wand that would create a force field around the creature. "At the very least, this should hold it."

Just then their communicators crackled, and Puppy's translated voice came through. "Update to the mission. Cyborg bacteria discovered. Taking the mushbug on board may cause problems for Earth later."

"Understood," said Geo. "But that means we can't even operate."

"See what you can find with external analysis. We might be able to work out what their secretions are actually made of, with what we've got."

Torus activated the wand and the mushbug froze, almost like it had been turned off. Their capture team quickly stood down and moved away.

"Yes, Puppy. "We will report as soon as possible."

There was a beep as Puppy disconnected, then Geo turned to Torus, holding up a drop. He'd noted the change in the light before Torus.

"I think I have some bad news."

Torus felt his body start to tingle, shift, and pull apart. "The suns are rising. Sorry, I need to return to the ship!" He immediately disappeared, and Geo turned to the extraction crew. "Alright team, let's see what we can find."

Moments later, Geo had his answer. He sent his team back for sterilization and called the ship.

"The nanite suits should have been able to unstick

from this glue," he said to the crew. "Either by changing frequency, or activating the scrubbers, but the glue has a subtle electromagnetic field that actually makes the nanites dormant. It could be why the Queen didn't let the mushbugs cover Cuddly with the glue. He wouldn't have been able to use his antennae."

"This is serious," said Puppy. "If any of the crew's suits are punctured while they're down there, the nanites may not be able to help them."

"Cuddly hasn't been glued, so he should be alright," said Torus.

"Spiney could survive for several minutes in a carbon dioxide environment if his suit ruptures, long enough for someone to repair it," said Amy. "But captain Hogart wouldn't last more than thirty seconds."

"We need to get them out of there as soon as possible. But we don't have any defense against the mushbugs."

"I have an idea," said Amy.

Outside their temporary jail cell, the mushroom-bugs continued to stick rocks to their undersides, bounce away, unstick them, and come back and get more. There were about ten of them and they seemed desperate to get into the cell.

"Aargh," said Hogart. "This is soooo boring!" He looked down on Spiney and Cuddly. Spiney still glued to the ground, Cuddly still curled up in a little ball.

They'd been there about an hour, and he knew that Cuddly's body needed to go every hour or so. He'd be ready to fire again any minute and start to get stressed in about thirty.

Unfortunately, Cuddly hadn't moved and even hadn't responded to Hogart's repeated calls.

"Cuddly, are you alright?"

"I think he's still in shock," said Spiney. "He hasn't damaged anything before."

"Well, it's good that he had his potty training away from the Stellar Flash!"

"Captain, I've been watching the aliens. When they approach, their undersides are wet and sticky. When the rock is attached, their bodies are dry."

"So, it's like an alkaline, acid combination. They secrete the alkaline to stick things, then the acid to dissolve it. How does that help us?"

"Cuddly's bladders, when released, produce a chemical mixture similar to acetone peroxide in a liquid form. His right bladder is mainly acetone, which might work against the glue. If he can somehow release only one bladder, he could get us both out of here!"

"Spiney, that's brilliant." Hogart turned the volume up on his suit. "Cuddly. Cuddly. "Come on, man, we need you."

Cuddly remained quiet.

"Officer Cuddly. Emergency evacuation!" yelled Hogart.

Cuddly suddenly uncurled and jumped to attention like a viper.

If Hogart could have clapped, he would have.

"Cuddly, you're back!"

Cuddly looked around, dazed. "What happened?"

"You exploded the wall, then went into a coma," said Hogart.

Cuddly looked around. "Oh, no." He began curling up again.

"No. No…Officer Cuddly! We need you to program your nanite suit to only allow one of your bladders to release."

"Not this again," said Cuddly, almost annoyed.

"It's an order. Your acetone side."

"I don't know what my acetone side is."

"Spiney says it's your right side."

"He's not an astrobiologist, and I'm not a doctor!"

"Aargh!" Hogart was starting to lose patience. "Cuddly, if you don't do it, we're all going to die."

Cuddly turned to Spiney, and without further argument, allowed the nanite suit to open the evacuation hole in his right side, and he began spraying over Spiney's spines.

Immediately, Spiney was able to unstick them from the ground. Cuddly worked around the rest of Spiney, freeing him from the floor.

When he was finished, Spiney got up and the sticky goo began to slide easily off him. His nanite suit seemed to spark and shimmer, then went to work completely sterilizing him.

"Captain, I think my nanite suit has been offline. Something in the glue. I think yours might be offline too."

Hogart gaped, then looked resigned. He was glad the air filters had continued to work. "Well, it looks like I'll have to go through this too, then. Alright Cuddly, now me. Program your nanites to project higher. I think you might be able to reach my head."

Cuddly set to work spraying Hogart. Even though Hogart had his helmet on, he closed his eyes. The memory of Cuddly's pissing leg would haunt him for a long time, so he wanted the least amount of memory to work with.

"Spiney, flash out of here and get back to the ship. Don't forget your final sterilization procedure. Cuddly, I need you here until the last possible minute as I might need to communicate. But if you can get me out in time, we leave immediately."

"Yes, sir."

Just as Hogart began to fall forward from the wall, the mushroom-bugs pushed the last remaining rocks away and bounced in.

"Spiney, go!" Hogart yelled. Spiney disappeared as the creatures piled on top of Cuddly and Hogart.

It wasn't long before they were before one of the queens again.

Spiney materialized in a featureless white room on board the Stellar Flash and was instantly sprayed with a concoction of chemicals while in his nanite suit, then blow-dried. A high-pitched hum began as a red light flashed up and down over him.

He made sure he wasn't blocking any part of his wide, spiky body as it was irradiated, and waited patiently until all the tubes and lights stopped flashing.

The AI's voice then said. "Stage One nanite suit sterilization procedure complete. Reintegrate nanite suit and begin Stage Two." Spiney's suit retracted to a band around his base, and a new chemical concoction began spraying him. "This is definitely my least favorite moment of any mission," he said.

The Queen's antennae were moving so fast it was almost impossible for Hogart to see, let alone for Cuddly to translate.

Hogart wondered what had happened to the other

queen. What was she doing? Was this the original queen or the new one?

"We witnessed your part with the many antenna disappear," said the Queen. "You must have the same ability. Give it to me."

Hogart laughed. "Over my dead body."

"We understand you value your parts. You helped your other part escape."

Hogart knew where this was going. He had hoped he wouldn't have had to deal with another cliché so soon on his tour of duty.

"And so," continued the Queen. "You will give me your technology, or I will separate your other part."

Hogart sighed.

"It's alright, captain. I'm not important. Leave me. There are many more in my clan, and I can transmit my consciousness to be with them and come back in a new body."

"What?" asked Hogart, surprised.

"These body-conduits are only temporary. I have many of them."

"Look, I'm pretty sure that my job is to make sure you don't die, no matter what body you have. So, forget about it. But thanks!"

Hogart shook his head. It didn't matter whether consciousnesses could be transferred, or even if someone was going to be reincarnated. The fact of the matter was that this life here, in this moment in space/time, was the only one that existed in all of infinity. If you leave it, it's not the same life. He wasn't going to get a new Cuddly. He wanted this one.

And besides, he had a backup plan.

"Alright, Queenie. I love my parts, and I wouldn't

want any of them hurt in any way. Release your heavies, and I'll give you my flash band. I'll even show you how to use it."

The Queen's antennae moved, and the bug holding Hogart unstuck itself. The bug holding Cuddly remained.

Immediately Hogart slid his silver fingers along his arm, trying to find the flash band within the nanite suit. The now dissolving glue made it difficult to feel the join but eventually he found it. He slipped his fingers under, and carefully typed in a code.

"What are you doing?" asked the Queen, suspicious.

"Typing in my passcode for you, otherwise it won't work for you or anyone."

"Very well."

Hogart finished and released the clasp. The silver flash system shifted to be outside his nanite suit without it compromising the internal atmosphere, and then slid off into his hand. He looked closely at it, then carefully walk-bounced closer to the Queen and held it up.

The flash band was more of a sleeve than a wristband. It contained several circuits, a read-out screen and an energy conversion system. The energy was eternal, taking its power from outside space/time. Such technology should never fall into the wrong hands, or antennae, and here he was giving it to someone who was not part of Earth government or the I.C.

He was going to pay for it at home if his plan didn't work.

"As a gift to show our goodwill, and our plan for inviting you into the trillion-civilization-strong Interdimensional Coalition, I hereby gift you with this flash band." Hogart bowed and handed the flash band to the Queen. To his surprise, the top two of her antennae flickered, and the flash band lifted out of his hand and floated in the air in front of it.

Telekinesis. But perhaps only the Queen had it, otherwise the mushroom-bugs would have used it on them.

"What does it do?" she asked.

"It is programmed with thousands of addresses across the universe. Scroll to go through the addresses, press to activate, press again to automatically return you to the previous location. Even though you have no hands, you have telekinesis, and that will work just as well."

He saw that the screen was flickering, and knew she was scanning through the addresses. He wondered if there would be enough time. Was she going to fall for the bait?

"There are so many. How can I choose?"

"Oh, they're all good, queenie. I couldn't possibly choose one for you. You should pick one and check it out, then come back and pick the next one."

The Queen kept scrolling, its antennae getting more agitated. "But none of these vibrations have additional information. I can't detect atmosphere or energy about the location. How can I…"

Just then, the Queen stopped. "What is that?"

"What?" asked Hogart, innocently.

"This one seems brighter. It has more energy around it."

"Oh, it's nothing. It's not really a place at all. Nothing special. A moon with lots of carbon dioxide, I think. Pretty boring place. I marked it to never go there again. I wouldn't go there."

The Queen's antennae flicked. "I don't think so. I'm sure you're trying to trick me. You want me to go to any of the other places, but this one has been marked as special. Hundreds of addresses and only this one is marked!"

"No, really Queen, there's nothing there. Honestly."

The Queen lowered the flash band to be directly in front of her, then slid it under herself. Moments later she disappeared in a bright flash of light.

The bugs around them suddenly fell to the ground, Cuddly's releasing him and collapsing. "Sir, they don't have access to their Queen anymore. The System has broken down."

"And now, the other Queen can take over this system."

"Divide and conquer?" asked Cuddly.

"Something like that. If we had had to see both at the same time, the plan wouldn't have worked. We got lucky."

Hogart was pleased to find that they hadn't had their shoes stuck to the ground this time. "Alright, get back to the ship, Cuddly. Spiney, I guess you've been listening to the conversation? Send me down another flash band."

Just then, a new flash band appeared and Cuddly disappeared. Hogart put his on and also flashed away, just as the other Queen bounced around the corner.

She immediately lifted her antennae high, and activated the mushroom-bugs again. "Now you are part of ME," she said. "And together, we will take over their ship and conquer their star system."

Chapter 9
Stellar Breeze

Heartness read through the reports. No other mushroom-bugs had appeared, and they couldn't track where that particular gold bug had disappeared to. They'd scanned as far as sensors could go, all the way out to Saturn's furthest moon Phoebe and to the center of the gas giant. No other ones detected.

She was slightly relieved that there wasn't an army of mushroom-bugs waiting to invade, but she was definitely concerned that it had had Hogart's flash band. Of course, she knew he could get more from the ship. They had thousands. But all the same, she thought she should shift to their reality briefly, just to check things out. They weren't due back for another few hours, but if they were in trouble, perhaps she could help.

She sighed. She knew she was just making excuses to get off the space station. Already getting itchy feet.

But there was something she was forgetting. Perhaps watching Watanabe's lecture would jog her memory.

She went back to her cabin and tuned into his stream. A few hours had passed since she had spoken to him, so perhaps her ship was almost complete. She shifted the image of his lecture to display on the wall, and when it appeared it was almost like he was in the room with her.

Hangar Sixteen was on the outer edge of level eight, Ring One. It was used for building new flash ships or running experiments on them. It was also the hangar that the Stellar Flash had been partly grown in. As the Stellar Flash was an equilateral triangular shape of approximately one kilometer on each side, it had just had one corner inside the hangar while the rest had been grown in space.

Thankfully, the ship she'd asked Watanabe to grow wasn't going to be that big. Being just a scout ship, it would barely fit her, let alone anyone else. Just enough to flash to another reality, then travel to a particular location. A mini triangle with a spherical seat inside.

If she knew exactly where the Stellar Flash was now, she'd be able to just flash there immediately. Unfortunately, she could only guess the orbit. And even then, if Hogart had discovered a threat, he might have moved the ship elsewhere.

She started the stream about halfway, then checked the time. An hour long and uploaded an hour ago.

It opened with parts of the hangar showing open space, and Watanabe standing in a force suit, with Saturn moving slowly past him. Watanabe had already created the energy template for her ship, and a faint yellow grid outline of what looked to be a smaller version of the Stellar Flash hung in the space of the hangar. The energy lines remained aloft as Watanabe directed a large tray of black chemicals to slide under them. The entire image wavered a bit as he was creating it remotely through a bubble reality. Heartness turned on the sound to hear what he had to say.

"This bit will be in the test, so pay attention. Now

that the EM field is holding the energy lattice in place, it is a simple procedure for the magnetic crystals to be attracted to the electromagnetic field and to react and grow. These are not going to just create a ship covered in large crystals like your grandmother might have owned. No, these are microcrystals with a structure that leaves barely any space between the atoms. Imagine interlocking hexagons on a subatomic level."

The chemicals in the tray swirled, and the black goo seemed to flicker and spark as it was attracted to the energy template like a magnet. Within moments the chemical had moved from slow seeping to rapid pouring, spreading across the energy shape at high speed. Heartness watched as the first 60-degree edge of the little ship rapidly formed.

"This tray of chemicals will create the shell of the entire ship, just microns thick but stronger than carbon nanotubes." Watanabe moved slowly in his suit and turned to another holographic board, writing calculations with his suited fingers. "Unlike our usual industrial techniques, creating these bonds this way makes the surface almost indestructible." He traced a few equations on the board as the black liquid continued to spread.

Moments later the liquid had completely disappeared from the tray and reached the last part of the energy template. Within seconds the liquid turned to something almost like icing, and then became completely solid and reflective, revealing a miniature version of the Stellar Flash, but with a black sphere in the center instead of a white one.

As soon as the ship had finished growing, it began to feel the artificial gravity of the space station, and floated to land on the surface of the hangar.

Watanabe reached over and flicked off a beam that had been streaming from a nearby terminal, creating the energy template. When the beam shut down, the ship shuddered a little then settled, finally able to exist on its own.

He watched the ship for a moment, making sure the newly created shell could remain without the energy grid, then deactivated the bubble reality. The ship stopped wavering and fully formed in the normal reality of the hangar.

He then strolled slowly over to it and marked an X on the edge of one of its corners.

Watanabe then moved carefully over to the other side of the hangar where a large tubular weapon sat against the wall, amongst industrial tools. "Now that the ship is complete, I will demonstrate how strong it is, with a plasma cannon." Watanabe picked up the cannon, raised it to his shoulder, took aim, then fired at the white X. When the plasma hit the shell of the ship, it deflected off into empty space, and the force of the contact skidded the vehicle across the floor towards the wall. The friction of the floor slowed the ship's movement and it came to a sliding stop, just before the airlock.

Watanabe immediately made some adjustments to the lecture camera, and zoomed into the X. "As you can see, not a scratch. If I had fired that at any part of the station, the plasma cannon would have destroyed walls one after the other and decompressed multiple sections. Of course, I knew which way the plasma would deflect for the safety of the base. Don't try this at home."

The Admiral was already surprised that he had done

that. Watanabe could be a bit erratic at times, but deflecting a plasma cannon into space when they had flight paths was irresponsible. Was anyone in danger? Admiral turned to the screen to check, then stopped. Of course, there weren't any. She'd cancelled them. She guessed Watanabe wouldn't have even thought to do that if there were ships in operation.

That's what she'd forgotten! To let everyone know that it was safe to resume flight paths. She should have set an alarm.

Watanabe continued speaking "So, what have we learnt? We learnt that we cannot use the Von Mises Yield Criterion to calculate…"

Heartness turned the stream off quickly and turned on her announcement system. "Alright everyone. Emergency is over. Back to normal operations. All ships can resume their original flight paths. All communications can resume."

She knew there weren't that many urgent communications between the space bases and Earth. They weren't being monitored 24/7. But if Earth had tried to contact her during the communications blackout, she'd soon know about it.

Perhaps that was something she could deal with later. She quickly sent a message to Patel, who had been assigned to fill in for her whenever she was away from the base, grabbed her bag and headed to hangar 16.

The atmosphere to the hangar had been restored, and she could see Watanabe's tight backside sticking out of the now open spherical section, no longer wearing his force suit. She admired it for a moment as the door closed behind her.

"Ahem," she said. She heard a bang and Watanabe pulled himself out of the sphere, rubbing his head.

"Ah, Vicky. You surprised me! I was just about to call you. Good timing. You're good to go."

"And the consciousness?"

"As far as I can tell, still a bit of a baby, but she'll be alright for you. I chose the resonant frequency closest to your alpha rhythms."

"That's excellent!" said Heartness, clapping her hands together. Then she pointed at her shoulder bag. "I'm all set!"

Watanabe stopped and looked at her directly. "But I haven't done any flight checks. The tests have all been responsive to individual stimulus, but not as a whole."

"Well, here's my chance to do that part of the test for you, Hiro."

Watanabe slid the rest of the way off the triangular ship and put out his hand towards it, indicating that it was all hers.

"If you insist. But I must make a formal protest."

Heartness laughed. "Of course! I'm very happy you're worried about my well-being."

"One other thing," said Watanabe. "Quite important, really. What are you going to call it? It's got a sphere so I think a name with Maru in it would be great. What about Stellar Maru?"

"Oh, I don't think we're ready for a name like that. Perhaps in a thousand years. It sounds a bit like a freighter ship, though. And I thought the tradition of ships made by Japanese ending in Maru disappeared decades ago."

Watanabe laughed. "I told you I was old-fashioned."

"In any case, I'm going to leave it up to the

consciousness of the ship to decide. She'll choose the best name based on both our feelings. I'll find out when I link."

"Just make sure you let me know, so that I can do some nice stenciling on the outside for you!"

"Will do. See you in a few hours, hopefully."

Watanabe stood back as Heartness hopped lightly onto the top of the triangle, then over to the petal-shaped control area.

She quickly slid into the soft and comfortable beige cockpit lounge seat and put her bag in the alcove behind her. She looked at everything approvingly. The ship had created itself to match her future body shape. She could use it for years and never worry about getting bigger.

She swiped across her blank console and watched as the petals closed back into a half sphere shape, waving goodbye to Hiro as they did.

Heartness looked around her as everything came online. The spherical screen showed the immediate outside of the ship. She could see Watanabe standing and watching patiently. To her left was the exit for non-flash shuttle craft, where she could just see a part of Saturn's bulk peaking from the edge.

She placed her hand flat on the white screen, and immediately the ship's controls and maps appeared on her mind view system. She swiped some virtual icons, entered an address, and the panel lit up with a countdown. She had quickly and easily completed the final integration with the ship. With it designed for her particular mental vibrational signature, no one else would be able to fly it.

She felt the tube behind her resonate, send its field out, locate a vacuum point, then begin the frequency adjustment. The ship hummed as the isolation field began to spread around it, and the cockpit started getting brighter. Little lightning sparks flashed around the inside of the console, then everything went white.

Outside the ship, Watanabe shielded his eyes as the bright light drained the color from everything around him, then he opened them again to see that the ship had gone. He waved a farewell to the empty space and left the hangar.

The hangar disappeared from the spherical view screen around her and was replaced with a brown and purple sky. Heartness immediately slammed her hand onto the white screen in front of her, pausing the ship in mid-air.

Somehow, she had appeared within the atmosphere of the planet. That was far too close.

She quickly set a course, speeding up time within the field of the ship, and the Stellar Breeze shot back up through slight wisps of clouds into a low orbit around the planet.

She adjusted the course and chose a stable orbit from where to begin scanning for the Stellar Flash.

She couldn't yet detect it. Perhaps they'd started moving away from the planet? She reset the coordinates and shot to a higher orbit.

Wait. Stellar Breeze? The consciousness had given herself a name! Heartness knew Watanabe would be pleased that at least one of the words he'd chosen had been kept.

She momentarily smiled to herself, before frowning again. Nothing was coming up on the proximity scanner. Surely, they were nearby?

The scanner continued scanning while she grabbed her bag and checked over the contents. After studying the images Patel had sent her, she decided that Hogart might need this.

She just hoped she wasn't too late.

Chapter 10
Mashbug

After going through the sterilization process and retracting their nanite suits, all of the crew had returned to the Stellar Flash Center. Even though he had only been gone a few hours, Hogart was glad to be back, and to have his flexibility back again. He didn't like nanite suits. He really looked forward to using force suits again, hopefully on the next mission. A lot less cumbersome.

He wasn't too sure why there was a giant piece of holographic rock in the middle of the Center, though.

Geo saw him looking curiously at it. "Amy's turn."

Hogart nodded. "Thanks Geo. Otherwise I would have probably lay awake trying to work that one out. What's the latest with the mushroom-bugs?"

"Mushbugs!" said Puppy.

"Alright, mushbugs it is. Amy?"

"Lots of news, sir. The star system is full of mushbugs. They use a cyborg bacterium that is quite virulent and has converted most of the outer atmospheres to carbon dioxide. Initially we thought it was too dangerous to take back to your reality, but I have since found your planet has had them before."

"Really?" asked Hogart, not quite following. Cyborg bacteria?

"When it appeared on your planet about 650 million orbits ago, it was destroyed by cyanobacteria, photosynthetic bacteria that creates oxygen."

Hogart waved his hand. "Oh, that! Yes, I learned about that in high school. Do you think the mushbugs had made it to Earth that long ago?"

"There is a possibility that they might have influenced the development of trilobites and horseshoe crabs," said Amy. "Though the trilobites of Earth evolved in a very different way to the mushbugs."

"It's possible that they transformed when shifting between the frequencies," said Geo. "Perhaps the mushbugs here are what the trilobites of Earth really looked like in this reality."

Hogart pondered this for a moment. He knew from his history lessons that trilobites were one of the most successful species on Earth, roaming the seas for over 270 million years. Humans had only been around in their present form for less than a million years. If the mushbugs ever made it to Earth again, he doubted the human race would last long.

He had a decision to make. He walked over to his station and stood looking at the crew. "AI, take this down. I officially declare that this area will be quarantined indefinitely, until such time as the creatures evolve to be mature enough to join the…"

"Captain," interrupted Amy. "Sorry to interrupt but permission to contribute another viewpoint."

"I didn't think this was a voting issue."

"I think, with the binaries affecting our judgement, that we should all be voting on this issue to make sure that any problems any of us might have are not influencing our decision."

Hogart stroked his chin. "Alright. What's your point?"

"Captain, they only captured you out of fear. They wanted our technology out of desperation. They have not as far as we can tell in recent times, killed many of their kind. And, from what we understand, they could all be from the same single alien anyway."

Hogart looked at her glutinous form incredulously. "Amy, my crew were threatened with death! One of the queens wanted our technology to fight others of her kind. There's evidence of a nuclear war having happened on the planet and, using your argument, the entire human race is from a single humanoid alien at some point."

"True, and at the meeting in 2050 which granted humanity a place in the IC, I was there using the same argument to defend your race!"

Hogart was silent. He hadn't any idea that Amy was so old, or that she had been such an important figure in their history. But could he really compare humans to mushbugs? How? They were almost like slaters. Or even cockroaches.

And he hated cockroaches.

"Geo?"

"I agree with Amy. We haven't found enough evidence yet to prevent them from joining. Or even for quarantining them."

Hogart looked about. Was he allowing his human side to influence his decision? An alien race treats him badly, so he won't give them first contact rights?

He sighed. Yes, he was doing exactly that.

"Alright team, I value your input. And being an emotional human that's just been captured, I'm more likely to judge negatively. Can we get a vote on it?"

All the aliens in the Center wanted to give the mushbugs another chance. Hogart was the only one unsure. "Right! Another chance it is. But I don't want to deal with the Queen down there. Should we investigate one of the other planets?"

"There is one thing that we haven't discussed yet, captain," said Spiney. "You gave one of the queens your flash band. That is secret human technology and must never leave your side. We're supposed to risk our lives to protect it. Yet, you just handed it over. We need to know whether we can trust *you*!"

The other aliens all turned and looked directly at Hogart, who immediately felt like he should be backing away. What…?

"Is this a mutiny, like Leafy did to Heartness? Are you being affected by the binary suns? In which case, perhaps we need to return to our frequency and get reinforcements."

"No captain," said Puppy. "This is a written procedure that you signed off on. We need to know why."

Hogart sighed again. He needed his crew on his side. "AI, replay Hogart suit recording approximately five minutes before sterilization procedure."

The Center screen showing the brown and purple planet blanked out and was replaced with a blurred, flickering, shuddering and fast-moving image. Hogart's helmet-camera's recording. His fingers were lifting the flash band off his arm, then programming an address. The address briefly flashed red, then settled with a mark next to it. He then spun the addresses, pulled the band completely off, and handed it to the Queen.

"Pause video," he said, then looked at the waiting aliens. "Well?"

"You sent her to Enceladus?" asked Torus. "Why?"

"I thought Heartness would find her and study her. If not, I would capture her when I got back. I'm sure she would have frozen almost instantly, the moment she arrived."

Behind Hogart, unbeknownst to him, a small spark had appeared on the surround screen, getting larger, slowly appearing as a yellow dot, then an oval.

"Captain. What if the Queen had realized your trick and activated the return immediately?" asked Spiney, looking at the screen behind Hogart.

"The flash band's default was human," said Hogart, thinking, stroking his chin again. "It wouldn't have been able to scan her full size properly to be able to transport her body to the correct coordinates. For a fast return, for security reasons it would transport what it could find, but the coordinates might be a little off."

"A few hundred kilometers off?" asked Geo, also looking at the yellow oval getting larger.

"Oh, probably. She might have ended up on another island."

"Well, I do think it might be possible she missed the island altogether," said Torus. "I believe it is highly likely she missed the entire planet."

"No, I'm pretty sure she's ended up on Enceladus."

"Don't you think we should check, just in case?" said Puppy, who had also noticed the image. "We wouldn't want that flash band floating around anywhere, would we?" Puppy's eyes were growing wider as the yellow oval became clearer.

"Oh, yes, that's probably a good idea. We could…," said Hogart. His voice tailed off as he realized that the aliens weren't actually looking at him. They were looking at something behind him.

He turned to see the yellow mushbug queen heading towards their ship at high speed.

"Shit! AI, get us out of here!"

"Activating flash drive to emergency coordinates," said the pumice stone.

The cylinder began to vibrate and turn white.

"I don't think this is going to work in time. The Queen will hit our isolation field before we flash. AI, just pilot us to another planet. Reduce our orbital velocity."

"Please state the coordinates for the planet location," said the AI, powering down the flash drive.

"Gaah. AI, the nearest one. Let's go." Even as he said it Hogart kicked himself. They were travelling at 3000 kilometers an hour. Even if he activated a fast time field around the ship, there was no way they could turn fast enough and take a new heading to avoid the bug.

"Activating interplanetary drive," said the AI.

As the gold mushroom-bug shot forward like a bullet, Captain Hogart knew that it was far, far too late.

The gold queen smashed itself across the outside of the Center, its broken shell pieces and internal goo spreading rapidly over the top of the camera images.

As the mashed mushroom-bug pieces slid down to conceal all of the surround screen, Hogart rubbed his face in dismay, knowing that he had been instrumental in the death of the leader of the planet. Not to mention the fact that now he couldn't see where they were heading.

His day couldn't get any worse.

Or so he thought.

Chapter 11
Puppy's Lament

I shut my six eyes briefly, recalling the recent scene on the bridge, while the other half of my mind took my body northward, navigating instinctively. My north eyes' memory viewed the brown and purple planet, mostly concealed by mushbug remains, while my south eyes' memory saw the human, the Captain, looking quite disappointed.

This was his first mission. New ship. New crew. New location. What did some humans say? Throw them in at the deep end and see if they sink or swim?

I believe the Captain has been sinking and hasn't started swimming yet. Though, if he had tried to swim in the sulfuric acid rivers on my world, dissolving would be the more correct word.

For many years now I have been studying humans and have learnt some of their body language. Their emotions and ours have some similarity, which is why many of us have been chosen to lead security detachments on the human ships. Though, I understand it is our massive bulk that tends to put fear into the hearts of many beings.

Usually males, in my experience. Most females I've met have been very impressed. I get offers from human females all the time, as it happens. Apparently, they like my really big tongue. I have no idea what they'd want to do with it though. Have a bath?

I'm not xeno though so it really doesn't appeal to me. And I'm really not into smooth skin. There's something really unappealing about a creature without thick hair on their bodies. Almost like touching their veins. Brr. And I must admit to finding some of the gorillas on Earth more attractive than the humans.

In any case, I'm rambling. The binary star system has been making it a bit more difficult for me to focus lately, and I'm very worried that I might make the wrong decision. But I must remain professional, so while we stopped in space and waited for the ship's nanites to complete collecting the mushbug queen's cells from the outside, with the captain's permission I flashed down to investigate the nuclear war evidence, and find some way to confirm or reject the idea that the mushroom-bugs were still actively war-like.

My excuse was that I wanted to be sure of my vote for their inclusion. My reason was simply to stretch my legs and give the other half of my mind some exercise. The Center might be tall enough for me to be there, but all exits are just a few clicks of my legs away. I make jokes to keep half my mind off it, but the Center being similar in size to a second brain punishment egg on my world does disturb me.

I had chosen to flash to the island where Leafy had previously attempted to reseed the world. For reference, we later found that Leafy had been dating a Floran male who had somehow convinced her that creating a Floran outpost here was a good idea. I assume the binary suns had also affected her thinking, not to mention her recent pollination, as she took over the ship and tried to launch seeds with the plan to convert the entire star system into a Floran colony.

It took quite a while for the nanites to restore

everything to how things were before, and the result of that was a massively detailed record of the island, created from the nanite network.

I put away my memories and reopened my eyes, pulling in the scenes around me.

My legs had taken me to the center of the island. Boulders, dirt, sand and rubble with occasional reflections off the patches of fused silica. A wasteland. Of course, beneath the surface there were billions of bacteria, teeming and converting various minerals into various other minerals. There were also some amoeba and a few insect-like creatures. So, the place wasn't as dead as it looked. Still, there wasn't anything there for me.

I pulled up the map on my nanite suit's HUD and located what I was looking for. A buried conical building not far away, almost invisible save for a point that stuck out of the ground. It didn't take me long to get there.

Glassy sand and rock-like segments of welded mushbugs littered the surface, broken only by pieces of building structures reaching upwards, as though struggling to take their last breath before the end.

Whatever they were made of, a nuclear bomb was enough to kill them. Though, there weren't that many remains further away from the flashpoint, so perhaps they survived anything other than a direct hit.

I shifted away a few boulders, then put my mouth down on top of the conical building and bit through the porous rock, removing the roof and spitting it to my east.

Inside was what I came to find, but like most places, humans tended to investigate, I couldn't enter.

I had brought a small drone with me, strapped to

my back, and I released it and sent it inside to record what it found.

The drone lowered itself into the conical building and turned slowly, shining a bright light on the walls, and revealing the scratches that had been left there, sending the image directly to my HUD.

A map of the base with a plan of attack, with arrows…

I looked at it in surprise. That can't be right.

The arrows were pointing at the structure, not away from it.

Had I misinterpreted?

The drone continued its search, and I knew I was correct. There definitely had been a nuclear attack, but not one that anyone would have expected. It was an inside job, with systems set up to attract the weapons to this position, to destroy whatever was there.

They had deliberately wiped themselves out.

Not at any point in the history of my world had any of us wanted to kill each other to such a degree. If what the AI had discovered was true, then a queen had made it here to prepare, before another queen had landed. Perhaps the first had sacrificed herself to destroy whatever civilization already existed to make space for the next mushbug family.

I checked the radiation readings. The attack had happened over a hundred years ago. The previous mushbug race would have been erased, and the new mushbugs taken over, bringing their culture and customs with them.

I retrieved the drone, picked up the roof with my mouth, and replaced it, sadly. Then I flashed back to the ship and submitted my report to the AI, returning to my station on the Center.

Unfortunately, discovering that the mushbugs had committed terrorist acts against members of their own race, and sacrificed themselves for it, has meant I've decided to withdraw my vote for them joining the I.C.

I just hope that the others would find a more compelling reason to offer membership.

Chapter 12
Geo's Metrics

My eye flap was shifted by the nanite suit to 'open' when it grew the spherical protection shield around me. I always found this disconcerting as I did not have the eyelids that some humans had, and the suit was not able to compensate by integrating with my other senses. For humans it would be like having something attached to their head that kept their eyelids open for several hours.

My eyes did not require the constant remoisturizing that humans' eyes did. Even so, I disliked this loss of control, and looked forward to when we could return to using force suits.

A further discomfort was the restriction on my usual method of movement. I used the various flaps on my body, or teardrops as Heartness liked to call them, to guide myself when I flew, floated or spun. I was equally comfortable flying in gas clouds, floating in ammonia seas, or rolling down a diamond incline, with my unencumbered physiognomy. But with the nanite suit I could only roll left or right. Rolling forward would cause some pain to my eye flap, requiring me to rely more on relocating by flashing.

It may be needless to put this in my report, but the humans require completion, and Jorjarar may find my story relevant.

In any case I had been tasked with answering a

question.

We had still not discovered whether the schools were military installations or not, and we hadn't had the chance to really investigate. Now that we were on the offensive, and we knew the mushbugs could see us anyway, Hogart thought that I would be the best person for the job. I could flash into and out of buildings quickly, checking scratch boards and translating conversations, instantly sending what I had found, and disappearing before being discovered. If I was discovered I would be quite quick at rolling away.

I decided to start with the conical building that had featured the scratch board with the Stellar Flash.

Of course, I thought it best not to enter that particular room again, considering what had recently happened to my colleagues, so flashed outside the bottom room first.

I was pleased to sense that no mushbugs were inside, and as the sky began to darken as the world turned to night, I hoped that they wouldn't be back again until morning.

I carefully rolled into the room, a slight crackling of my suit touching the hard ground the only sound I made.

This room contained many more rectangular resting pads than the others, was a lot wider, and the scratchboard filled a lot more space on the wall. In fact, there were several of them. And here, I could see that the information on the board was a lot more complicated. There were symbols that were small on one side of the board and larger on the other which suggested some kind of progression of mathematics.

As I had been designated an astrophysicist by the humans I felt that I had the knowledge to be able to easily interpret any mathematical construct, no matter what the language. My translator would soon have it worked out.

I quickly found that, without even the slightest similarity in mathematical symbols, there was no way I could understand the scratches in front of me.

I went to the next board and reached out my senses, not only detecting the scratches that were on the board now, but the ones that had been there before and had been erased or written over.

On the surface, the second board contained nothing of interest. A few more scratches describing geographical features of the planet. It was what was underneath that was more interesting.

Erased just a few days previously were scratches of the star system, and I was surprised to sense that the mushroom-bugs actually knew a lot more about the planets in the area than we had learnt from our orbs.

The hidden diagram showed thirty planets aligned along the elliptic. This was amazing in itself as the one the furthest away was trillions of kilometers distant. How could they have known that?

But what really struck me as strange was that each of the planets was larger than the last – slowly increasing in size until the secondary binary star. There almost seemed to be a natural progression. The increments between the size of the planets were even. Not only that, but the gaps in orbit followed the humans' Titius-Bode rule, of spaces between subsequent planets' orbits to continue to double, the further out you go.

Of course, there was no way that the scratch board could include all 30 planets to scale, but I was able to reinterpret a bent-shaped symbol to indicate repeated sections of missing space.

Was there some kind of cultural significance in the increasing size of the planets, perhaps symbolizing that they were closer, or were they really equally larger than each other?

I quickly discounted the first theory when I discovered that the planet that was two away from the first star was marked with a symbol where the others weren't. As this was the one that we were on, and the next planet was still larger, it suggested there really was a progression in size.

I realized I was becoming distracted by this drawing. The astrophysicist in me could roll back and forth for hours, applying various mathematical formula from around the universe to understand the scratching. Forcing myself away, I sent the enhanced image to the ship, then carefully rolled to my left and out of the empty room.

As I rolled up the ramp to the next section I wondered why, even though school was over, there weren't mushbugs guarding the area. Were they just slaves to the Queen? With the main queen gone, would they simply forget their allegiance, and then forge a new one, following new rules and regulations with the new queen? I really could not understand this idea of aliens simply accepting a change in the way society was ordered, just like that. Perhaps I could compare it to something completely alien and incomprehensible, like letting a government of representatives run your life for you rather than running your life yourself. I had difficulty imagining a society like that.

It is possible that my inquiries would be for naught as, even if this had been a general education school, the new queen may change it into a military one anyway.

I rolled into the next room and was once again surprised by what I found. Scratches of the ring of carbon dioxide volcanoes, accompanied by lines in arcs from the volcanoes to the sky.

Were they teaching the mushbugs how to enter orbit using volcanoes? I quickly calculated the launch velocity needed. Even though this planet had low gravity, and a mushbug shell was quite strong, the internal pressure and release of carbon dioxide would not be enough thrust for low orbit, let alone set them on a suitable trajectory for another planet.

Our recent translation of the queens' conversation suggested this possibility, but to know that they were actually teaching this idea to the younger mushbugs suggested it was not a rare act.

It was then that I realized exactly what they were teaching them here. Information about the star system. Information about how to escape it and go elsewhere. It was a classic case.

I knew now what the conical building and, in fact the school as a whole, was for. There was no need for me to investigate the other buildings. I am sure they would all be the same. I activated my flash band and returned to the ship.

"Immigration?" asked Hogart incredulously, once Geo had given his report. "Are you kidding me?"

"I am sorry, Captain, I have not learnt that particular skill from Puppy as yet. I have begun taking lessons from him but…"

"Sorry Geo. It's just an expression. I can't believe it."

"Everything matches, sir," said Puppy. "I guess the third room is probably for contingency measures, risks or potential threats."

"But why teach the black and brown ones? I'm pretty sure that they're almost like slaves here. They can't go anywhere."

"Why teach all your humans how to do mathematics when most of them don't use algebra after the age of 19?" asked Amy.

"Good point," said Hogart. "But, I thought only the Queen was capable of migrating to the other planets. The other mushbugs don't have telekinesis, so they wouldn't be able to guide themselves anywhere."

"Well, we don't know that for certain, so there's every possibility that there are different levels of mushbugs we don't know about."

Hogart thought about this for a moment. Mushbugs that might have the skills of the Queen but weren't gold-colored. It's amazing they lasted this long with a queen in charge. If they had her skills and realized it, there'd be an overthrow at some point. Hogart wondered why the Queen didn't simply abdicate and give the world to the mushbugs. If she did that, they could develop in their own way and push society further forward.

"Thank you for your report Geo," Hogart said. "We've got our question answered. Not an education school, not a military school, but a school that enables mushbugs to either help plan for, or be involved in, an escape to a new planet."

Just then the AI appeared. "Sir, the collection process is almost complete. Set course?"

"Let me think about that," said Hogart. "I'd like to go and look at her remains a bit more closely. Pay my last respects, and all that. I can't believe she came all this way to just be mashed against our screens. Not with her telekinetic abilities."

"Yes, sir."

Hogart looked about the room. Going and seeing the Queen's remains wasn't the most exciting job, but he best take someone along that can at least distract him a little. He really should take his astrobiologist with him.

"Amy, join me when you're done."

She flicked a watery arm to confirm and continued finalizing her report. He had tasked her with working out the next best planet to visit. She'd know soon enough.

And then, perhaps, they'd finally get a First Contact situation happening for this star system.

If the death of the Queen didn't cause the entire mission to come crashing down around him first.

Chapter 13
Murder on the Stellar Flash

The nanite cleaning system had collected all the remaining pieces of the mushroom queen and had stored them in the Stella Flash's quarantine area.

Two vats full of a grayish fleshy liquid sat in one part of the room, with another vat full of gold-colored chitinous pieces.

Hogart looked through the window at the vats in dismay. Things had not quite gone to plan. And now, here he was, with the dead body of the Queen of a world that he'd planned to forge a First Contact agreement with.

From what he remembered, this queen was desperate to go elsewhere, and give her world to her children. The new queen, however, just wanted to take over everything. Could she be trusted? Could he start again with the new queen?

He was glad that with his advanced recycling systems he only had to eat once a day. If he would have had to have eaten something now, that vat of slimy-gray, soupy, mucus-like corpse would have turned him off his lunch.

He heard a squelching sound, and Amy slid up to form a slightly feminine shape beside him. Even though she was a greenish glutinous blob that he could see through, she knew the exact curves to use to excite even the most reticent and conservative straight male human. Momentarily distracted, Hogart looked her up and down, then turned back to the quarantine screen. He couldn't do anything right now.

"You look a little stressed, Captain," said Amy. "I've been trained in human massage techniques. Perhaps I can help you, in your cabin."

Hogart turned to her and raised an eyebrow. "Well, Amy, I'm very flattered, but I read the AI's medical reports of the team. It confirms what we all suspected, that we're all being affected by the binary suns' electromagnetic spectrum. You, in particular are, shall we say, feeling a bit more, you know…"

Amy twisted in her translucent puddle body, attempting to use coy body language. "Whatever do you mean, captain?" then she squelched down and back up again, becoming a pole of goo. "You're right. With my form, no one can resist, so I'm used to taking it anytime I want it, which has only been when I want it. Now I'm wanting it when I don't usually want it, so you're right to reject me."

"No, Amy, I'm not rejecting you! I'd love to know what it feels like to have you explore my skull. I understand it's a hundred times better than ASMR. I'm just saying this isn't the time. Anyway, did you decide on the planet?"

Amy twisted and became a more roundish blob.

Perhaps stretched means disappointed, round means neutral, thought Hogart.

"Yes, it means going a bit closer to the binary stars though, but the next planet has gravity closer to that of Earth, and has a higher oxygen content, too."

"Great! As soon as we get back we'll head there. Many thanks."

"There's something else. I've been analyzing the

pieces of the Queen," began Amy. "It looks like she's not what she appears to be."

"How so?"

"The pieces of her upper shell in the vat on the left. They didn't break. They separated."

Hogart used his fingers on the window and it complied by enlarging the image of the vat. He zoomed in on the pieces sticking out of the lid. He could tell that the edges of each of the pieces looked to be able to interlock with the other pieces. He started back from the window in surprise.

"But that means, when she said the other mushbugs were part of her, she wasn't talking about them being part of her family, she meant that everything was made up of her parts. So, all the mushbugs are really tiny pieces joined together to make larger ones!"

"The creatures are greater than the sum of their parts," said Amy.

Hogart began pacing in front of the window. "So, even if we speak with the Queen, and request first contact, and she agrees, she's not really representing the planet. She's just being a composite creature that wouldn't exist if all the creatures were separated. The real creatures on the planet are those pieces in the vat."

"Yes, captain. It means that this star system is full of billions of life forms that come together to create greater lifeforms. But they don't have enough intelligence to have first contact separately."

"So, it's impossible for them to agree to terms because, as soon as they separate again, they would forget what they had originally agreed to."

Amy's form twisted again. Hogart assumed it meant agreement.

He looked at the gold pieces again and could see them lose balance and fall further into the vat. Then, as the hairs began to rise on the back of his neck before his thoughts had fully formed, he realized that he had felt absolutely no vibration.

"Amy," he said, backing away from the glass, "I think the pieces are on the move. AI, activate a containment force field around the vats. Keep them separate."

A beam of light enveloped the vats, and the three containers were surrounded by separate force fields.

"That should hold them," he said. "Well, Amy. It looks like we have another problem. Let's get back."

Puppy had just completed the scan of the Queen's trajectory and had some good news for the captain when he arrived at the Center. "We've located your flash band."

"That's great!"

Puppy zoomed in on it turning slowly in space, as a drone reached out grasping arms and collected it.

"AI, snapshot that image and zoom it," ordered Hogart.

The AI complied, and a paused image of the turning underside of the flash band appeared on the forward screen.

"Well, Amy? What do you think?" Hogart pointed at the quite obvious yellow hexagon stuck in the exact center of the underside.

"Interesting," Amy said.

"Do you think the pieces can store memory, or even consciousness?" asked Hogart.

Just then Puppy clacked his legs and came over

from his station. "Captain, you haven't heard the Queen's conversation!" He called up the previously recorded translation, and replayed it for Hogart, Spiney and Cuddly.

"So, the new queen has all the old queen's memories, even though they had separated into individuals," said Hogart, rubbing his chin. "Perhaps each piece stores memories in the DNA?"

"If that's true," said Amy, "Then first contact could still happen as others of the race would remember it, even in piece form."

"Sir, I advise caution," said Puppy. "I suspect that each piece has an urge to join with other pieces until a complete creature is made. Don't go near any separate pieces. Especially not any pieces deliberately stuck on the underside of your personal flash band."

"Good point, Puppy."

"And I believe it may be just the queens that can remember," added Torus. "Otherwise, why have a school for the mushbugs?"

"Another good point. Thank you, Torus."

Just then an alarm began to sound throughout the ship.

The block of stone flashed red. "Quarantine breach."

Hogart looked at the AI's hologram in surprise. "How on Earth…?"

One of the analysis robots stood in the empty quarantine room, scanning for any residue of the Queen. This time Hogart had asked Spiney to come with him, and they were both watching through the quarantine window.

"Not a single cell remains," it said. "We will unpack more androids and continue microscanning."

It was a hermetically sealed room. There was no way out.

"I think I'm forgetting something," said Hogart, looking at the empty room. "Even at the microscopic level there was no way that the Queen could have got out of there."

"Unless she phase-shifted."

Hogart slapped his head. "Of course. She learnt that from us. We were wandering around her school unseen. She must have worked out how to do it."

"And now she's on board, wandering around, just outside our frequency. We have no way of knowing where she is and what she's doing," said Spiney.

"Well, this is a dynamic ship and she'd be struggling just to stay on board phase-shifted. She could fall through the floor, ceiling or even out the side if we changed direction." Hogart stopped then and looked at the ceiling. He could sense something but couldn't see it. He looked back at Spiney.

"So, what do you suggest, captain?"

"I suggest we let her follow us until we can work out her plan, and let's give her some information so that she doesn't feel completely left out."

"Are you planning another role play?" asked Spiney.

Hogart showed his teeth in a huge grin, suddenly understanding that Spiney had guessed their introduction ceremony had had a little play acting. His respect for his first officer increased.

"That look means smile, and happiness, doesn't it?" said Spiney. "You're not about to attack me?"

"Well, I'm not a lion!" laughed Hogart. "Let's get started."

As Hogart and Spiney moved away, a faint outline appeared along the ceiling, floating outside the quarantine room window.

The outline became stronger and then a gold creature appeared, floating upside down, its antennae flicking and twisting, its body undulating silently. It slowly disappeared again, leaving a faint warped outline in the air.

Hogart was at the end of the corridor as a Floran guard, its dark green leaves held wide, made its way towards the quarantine room. Hogart pointed to the corridor, making some hand movements, and the guard lifted a leaf in confirmation, then headed towards the area.

The creature watched all this, seeing the movements of the aliens below it as waves of energy. Some waves were larger, some smaller. Two waves headed away from it, while one headed towards it.

It would investigate the single wave.

It materialized again, its gold form filling the entire space of the ceiling. It flicked its antennae as the plant alien got closer.

The Floran began waving its fronds and leaves in surprise as it began to float off the floor. Leaves and branches snaked out from its body as it attempted to grab the walls to stop itself floating higher. It looked up, finally realizing it was in danger, then began screaming.

The quarantine room glass splashed with green, and the screaming stopped.

Hogart and Spiney heard the scream and rushed back down the corridor, but Hogart held his arm out to prevent Spiney from going further. "Florans don't just randomly explode for no reason, do they?" he asked.

"No, sir. They do not."

Hogart lifted his flash band. "Attention all crew members. Hostile intruder alert. Activate nanite suit protocol 1."

The message reverberated up and down corridors around the ship.

Alien crew members in various areas of the ship looked at each other in surprise, then quickly moved away from wherever they were sitting or standing and began hitting, slapping or otherwise activating their flash bands.

Hydroponics Lab 12, a Floran and a sphere activated their suits, and they began growing around them.

Robot Repair Workshop 8. Three humanoid researchers and one hairy bear like creature with six arms stood, and their nanite suits began growing.

In the food hall, several crew members of various sizes and shapes had their suits almost complete, with bubble helmets appearing over their heads.

In the Center, the crew were watching their spacesuits grow around them, though protocol 1 meant one slight difference. Along the side of the suit, a firearm also grew. A mini plasma cannon.

Across the Stellar Flash, the crew grew their

armaments and got ready to protect themselves.

In a small egg-shaped room that looked a bit like a library, Jorjarar was reviewing reports and committing them to memory, pacing back and forth, his massive bulk swinging almost like a pendulum. "And then the captain discovered that the creature had escaped the quarantine area. And then the captain discovered that the creature had escaped the quarantine area," he said, then referred to the screen again.

Then he saw it. A flashing light on his console.

"What?" he muttered, annoyed. "I'm never to be disturbed! I'm not to be involved. How can I do my work with all these constant interruptions?!"

Grumpily, he pressed a button and the captain's voice came through. "Jorjarar. The AI has advised me you haven't activated your suit yet. You must activate nanite suit protocol 1."

A faint oval shape shifted through the wall behind him, and moved up, while Jorjarar's attention was focused on the communications system.

Jorjarar was getting upset. "But I'm the Storyteller. I can't get caught up in any fights. I'm just here to observe, and you're going to protect me. I've got to memorize everything! Otherwise, you won't have proper records in Frequency Zero!"

A gold antenna began to curl down from the ceiling. Then more antennae, and finally the first section of the Queen appeared.

"Jorjarar, the creature could be anywhere," said Hogart's voice. "If you don't put your suit on then there'll definitely be no records in Zero!"

Just then the Storyteller noticed that his feet were off the ground. He turned his head up, saw what was there, and screamed.

"Jorjarar? Jorjarar? Are you there? Shit."

As the light from the communications console disappeared, blue blood dripped onto the surface.

In Astrophysics Research Bay 4, a small yellowish insect-like humanoid with big black eyes hit his flash band several times, but the nanite suit wouldn't activate. He was getting agitated.

He clicked, and his translator said, "What is this?"

Behind him, an outline began to appear in the wall and the shape slid upwards.

"Of course!" he said, not seeing the intruder, and put his hand on the screen. "Pause project. Disable EM field block."

He happily hit his arm buttons again and was pleased to see his suit begin to grow from his feet.

Unfortunately, it was far too late. Before his suit had even reached halfway, he was pulled into the air, screaming.

As his scream was abruptly cut off, a splash of yellow hit his monitor.

Hogart and Spiney rushed back to the Center. "Situation?" yelled Hogart.

"A third crew member's life signs have been terminated. Astrobiology research room. Everyone else has their nanite suits protecting them now."

"If the Queen continues in a straight line, she will end up here," said Torus.

"Not if I can help it," said Hogart. "Are there any large rooms between here and the Quarantine room?"

"There's the scout craft hangar bay," said Geo. "We've got force fields and guns. We could force it there."

"It can phase shift. We need it to want to go there," said Hogart. "I have a plan."

The Queen floated over the alien's body, twitching its antennae and moving pieces about with its thoughts. It floated an arm and put it against its underside, but it wouldn't stick. It fell to the ground again. The gold bug then lifted the head and placed it against her shell, but that didn't stay either. Its antennae flicked and the pieces fell to the floor, hard.

The Queen was angry.

It phase-shifted and disappeared, floating through the doorway and into corridor three. It would find the leader.

"So, Cuddly, are you ready?" Hogart had taken his position, as others had taken theirs.

"Yes, sir."

"AI?"

"Cameras will project Cuddly's translations to every screen on the ship," said the AI.

"Alright, let's start."

Cuddly's nanite antennae had grown again and had begun to translate.

"Well, team, I'm really sorry that this has happened," began Hogart. "I had no idea that the Queen would have been hurt when I gave her my flash band. I really want to see her again. I think I might have upset her."

"Yes, we must make amends. We should give her the technology." said Spiney, playing along. "She seemed a very nice alien. We should help her."

"I will go to the largest room here, and I will go by

myself so that the Queen will feel safe. I will wait for her. We can talk there," said Hogart.

"By yourself?" asked Torus. "Are you sure?"

"Oh, yes, Torus. I am sure. I will go and wait for the Queen there by myself. I trust her."

Hogart then made a cutting movement with his hand, and Cuddly knew this meant that he should turn off the translation. His antennae retracted.

"Alright, team, do you think that will work?" asked Hogart.

"Captain," began Amy. "Do you think the Queen would have pulled apart those three crew members if she could be trusted? I'm not even sure she is the same queen."

"What do you mean?"

"Well, she's the confrontational type. She's not going to hunt in shadows. I think she's not all there."

"You think she's gone crazy?"

"No, I think she's missing a piece. That piece that is stuck to the flash band. I think we need to give it to her."

Hogart thought about this for a moment. "Then there are two possibilities. One: Restore the Queen and offer a First Contact contract, or Two: vaporize her as soon as the opportunity arises."

"I don't like option two," said Amy.

"Neither do I," said Hogart.

The Queen watched the antennae of Cuddly moving and heard the noises that the other aliens were making. The leader wanted to meet her nearby. She reached out with her sensors and detected various areas of atmosphere of different temperatures. One area had more temperature fluctuations than most and contained a lot more atmosphere. She phase-shifted and moved through the walls towards the location.

She would wait for the leader there. Perhaps this one had the knowledge she needed.

Hogart checked his tubular firearm, swiping the display screen with his left hand, making sure it was fully charged.

He looked at the flash band in his right hand. It had been disabled and surrounded by a crackling forcefield. The gold hexagonal shape was still attached to the base. If that gold piece was still alive, he didn't want it trying to merge with him. He held it out carefully as he headed for the scout hangar.

"Captain," transmitted Puppy. "Amy has analyzed the medical reports and confirms the Queen wanted the victims' brains."

Hogart stopped and shuddered. "Are you kidding me? Surely brain sucking aliens are a myth?"

"Everything checks out. The Queen pulled them apart to get to their brains."

Hogart thought for a moment. "Okay, let's think logically. Do any of the aliens have anything in common? What if she was looking for something specifically?"

There was silence as Puppy scanned the reports of the victims.

"Captain, they've all had pilot training."

Hogart closed his eyes and opened them. So much for pilot of the week. The Queen must have wanted the knowledge so that she could take the ship.

"Puppy, assign extra security to anyone with pilot training, and contact me the moment you know where the Queen is. If she doesn't turn up at the hangar, we might need a few pilots as bait."

"Yes, captain."

Spiney and Torus stood on guard outside the entrance to the scout hangar, while Hogart carefully entered, his nanite suit humming at full strength. He quickly looked about the metallic area. A section opened onto space enclosed by a forcefield, walls a few minutes' walk to either side. Similar to the main hanger on X-1a where the Stellar Flash was built, but a little smaller.

Even so, the area was quite large. Big enough for an emergency scout ship. They didn't need them as they had flash bands, but perhaps a short-range ship would be useful to have. Especially for situations where drones couldn't do the work. He'll speak with Heartness about it when he got back.

If he got back.

He looked along the floor, at all the walls, along the ceiling and even behind the door to the hangar, pointing his arm around like a secret agent searching for hidden spies.

There was no gold alien mushbug Queen creatures hiding anywhere.

Was she going to take the bait?

Was she setting her own trap?

"Hey, queenie, queenie, queenie. You know, I've got pilot training, too. You can't be a captain without it."

Suddenly, he felt something drip onto his suit back, the sensation being translated directly to his skin.

Then, what sounded like a rattling, clicking, gurgling growl came from all around him, getting louder.

He looked up and to his horror, saw the Queen

fully phase shift into his reality, its six sharp, blue, green and yellow bloodied pincers reaching for him.

Legs?

He cried out as the pincers yanked him up into the air.

Since when did the mushbugs have legs?

"Spiney, Torus. I need you!" Hogart yelled, struggling against the fearsome pincers.

His two crew members ran into the hangar area and took aim, but the Queen was throwing Hogart around so fast, that they couldn't get a clear shot.

Hogart realized she was trying to pull his arms and legs apart. "I said I come in peace," he yelled. "Not pieces!"

The Queen had now got a grip on both his arms and legs, and he was spread-eagled underneath her.

"This one does not have ridges," said Torus.

"Yes, I can see that, Torus."

"Your plan for the nanite suit to resist being torn apart by her glue body, appears to have become unstuck."

"Oh, a joke. Very funny, Torus," gasped Hogart. "I think you've been hanging around Puppy too much."

"Sir, the flash band. Give it to her," said Spiney, as Hogart continued to fight against the pincers.

"What do you think I'm trying to do?"

Suddenly his suit began making a scratching noise, and five antenna grew out the top of it. The Queen stopped moving.

"Cuddly!" acknowledged Hogart. "Tell her I mean her no harm and want to give her her missing piece."

The Queen's antennae flicked in response. "We together."

"I think she means she wants to merge with you

Captain."

"What? No! I mean, I'm flattered, and I respect your life choice, but I'm really not that way inclined."

"No, captain, she wants to put your pieces into her pieces."

"I know what she wants!" Hogart finally got one arm free. He pulled the flash band out of the bag and threw it at the Queen.

The wristband turned, the gold piece on the inside glinting as it spun through the air. It struck the edge of the Queen's shell and…

…bounced off and crashed to the floor.

Hogart looked down at it in dismay. *Well, that didn't work.*

"Queen. Your other piece, it's on the ground. Grab it and you'll be complete again."

"You complete me," said the Queen's antennae.

"Yes, I will, sure, just reach down and get that flash band and put it on."

The Queen ignored him and pulled him further into herself. He could see her exterior shell flickering at its edges, and then it began to grow. The shell began stretching and surrounding him.

"Guys, shoot now. Otherwise she'll cocoon me inside and I don't want to think about what will happen next. And no head jokes please!"

Spiney and Torus began firing at the Queen, but their bolts reflected off her hard exoskeleton.

Hogart felt the pull of the Queen's legs stretching him against her body, saw the shell almost completely envelope him, and heard her make a gurgling, rasping noise, almost triumphant.

As even his nanite suit couldn't cut through the encroaching blackness, his last thought was how was

he going to get out of this one?
   Was this the end?

Chapter 14
We Come in Pieces

Just as the last gold chitinous piece locked in place, and Hogart felt his nanite suit struggling against the talons of the Queen, a bright energy began to filter through the shell.

He looked in wonder as the hexagonal pieces of the bug became brighter, the pulling of his arms and legs stopped, and the section near him seemed to be dissolving.

Were they cutting through with laser torches?

Suddenly, he was free falling. The shell, then the pincers, then the body of the creature collapsed into so many hexagonal bricks around Hogart as he crashed onto the hangar floor, the remaining pieces of the Queen showering around him.

Hogart groaned, got up slowly, checked he was still in one piece, then dusted himself off. He looked at Spiney and Torus. "That was amazing! How did you do that?"

"Ahem," came a voice. Hogart recognized it and spun around to see a black triangular scout craft, and Admiral Victoria Heartness holding some kind of forcefield weapon.

"Admiral! I'm so glad to see you!"

"I heard you were having some problems with a leggy blonde, again. Thought I'd drop by to help out."

Hogart raised his eyes at the joke but was definitely

happy she appeared at the right time.

"It's not what it looks like," he said with a grin.

Heartness laughed. "Well, you better fill me in."

After they had headed back to the Center, and Heartness had been brought up to date, she informed them of the Queen's appearance on Enceladus.

"The only thing I can't figure out," she said, "is why time had been reversed for it. That's never happened before with a frequency shift."

"The flash address didn't send her to a vibrational resonance cavity to create a perfect connection to Zero, but it shouldn't have reversed time for her," said Hogart.

"The only thing I can think of is that the binary suns are having random effects on just about anything," said Amy. "We were affected by them last time. Perhaps they are creating temporal anomalies as well."

"But we shouldn't be affected by them at all," said Heartness. "There are thousands of binary star systems. We've been to many of them in Frequency Zero and One. Why is this one so different?"

Hogart nodded. They needed to figure this out. If there were temporal anomalies being created, their mission might be at considerable risk. He didn't want to suddenly put his hand in the air somewhere and have it age ten years.

"AI, prepare a couple of probes and send them to the stars' coronas," said Hogart. "Let's see if there really is something special about these suns that our remote sensors can't detect."

The AI set her production systems to work and two more probes flashed away.

"One more thing," said Heartness, turning to the crew to get all their attention. "We're heading to the most populated planet, we're investigating the stars, we're probably going to put the Queen back together, with either the potential of war or first contact success, and all these things are happening without any proper record being made. Not to mention the loss of three crew members."

Hogart raised an eyebrow. "Do we have to?"

"The people at home need to know."

Hogart frowned. He knew what this meant. It was time to get a new Storyteller. He suddenly realized how freer he'd felt since his thoughts were no longer being monitored. He had hoped he could wait until the mission was over.

He sighed. "So be it. Admiral, I've never resurrected a Storyteller. You can show me."

Just as they were about to leave the Center, Spiney called to them.

"Sir, ma'am, we need to delay a Storyteller for the moment. There is a much more serious situation that you're both needed for. On screen."

Hogart and Heartness rushed back to look at the screens while Spiney continued speaking. "I believe the Queen wasn't just searching for pilot's brains. I think she was trying to keep us occupied."

Hogart rubbed his face when he saw them.

Heartness just looked incredulous. "I don't believe it.

"Believe it," said Hogart. "It looks like the black and brown mushbugs have telekinetic abilities after all."

On the surround screen, a cloud of shapes were speeding towards the ship, and were almost upon them.

"AI. Evasive maneuvers. Get us out of here."

"Negative," said the AI, just as the first mushbug landed on the ship. They could hear the slight thump, thump, thump, as more mushbugs hit the surface and stuck fast. These did not break up like the Queen. They remained intact and began to cover the surface of the sphere.

"Negative?" asked Hogart.

"Ship maneuverability compromised by telekinetic abilities of the mushbugs," reported the AI.

The image around them quickly showed the mushroom-bugs covering the ship on the top, bottom and sides.

"Analysis confirms that while we were chasing the Queen around the ship, the volcanoes launched platforms of mushroom-bugs into orbit," said Torus.

"Great. That's just great," said Hogart, irritated. "So, the Queen has been distracting us. She already had a plan in place for when we returned. She must have simply activated it the moment she first captured us on the planet. Even when I sent her to Enceladus, things kept moving. Keeping us distracted while everything came together."

"It looks that way," said Amy.

More thumps and, once again, the surround screens were obscured by mushbugs.

"Oh, this is just terrific." Hogart at the screen. "Now we can't even see our next destination."

Just then the room lurched, the ship turned dramatically, then its angle shifted, momentarily disrupting the internal gravity. Hogart had to hang onto his console to stop from falling.

"Well, apart from the fact that we have thousands

of ways to know where we're going, I don't think we need to see anyway," said Puppy. "I'm sure we can all guess where they're taking us."

Chapter 15
Clouded

"Report!" yelled Hogart, as he began to feel buffeting against the bottom of the Stellar Flash.

"Re-entry within tolerances," said the AI.

"Re-entry? Hasn't anyone the ability to control this ship?"

Heartness went over to him. "YOU didn't choose a pilot." She poked him in the chest hard enough to hurt. "And now you have no control over the Stellar Flash."

"The AI can pilot it." Hogart turned to the stone in the middle of the room. "AI, get us back into orbit."

"Negative," said the AI. "Telekinesis override."

Hogart looked at Heartness and shrugged. "Even if I had a pilot, they wouldn't be able to override the telekinesis."

Heartness turned away from him, slightly annoyed, but she knew he was right. Even so, he was starting to make her angry. Was she getting possessive of her old ship and crew? She turned to Amy. "Any ideas?"

Amy replaced one of the panels of the surround screen with her station's connection. A white box image appeared. She swiped across her screen, leaving bubbles on the surface, and they went to work creating the image in her mind, before sliding back across the panel and rejoining her body.

"What are we looking at?" asked Hogart as two sets

of wave line images began to appear, one set wider than the other.

"Telekinetic wavelength comparisons," said Amy. I've analyzed the Queen's ability to pull you up in the hangar, and I've analyzed the mushbugs on the outside of the ship. Different telekinetic wavelengths."

"How different?"

"The Queen's are much stronger. The other mushbugs need to operate as a group and be much closer to have any effect."

"So, hundreds of mushbugs equals one queen. Well, we have hundreds out there. So we're still having the same problem."

The ship jerked as it hit an air current, and a whining noise filled the air.

"Are they going to just let us fall?" asked Heartness.

"It is likely they believe that they can simply put everything back together again," said Geo.

"We're not Humpty Dumpty!" said Hogart. "And, as I recall, things didn't work out well for him either."

"Captain, we barely have minutes left to get control of this ship before it's too late to avoid the ground," said Heartness. "Do something!"

Hogart looked around the crew. "Come on, guys. Think of something."

Then he looked at his first officer. "You've been very quiet, Spiney. Any ideas?"

"I've been monitoring the situation…," began Spiney.

"Yes…"

"…and reviewed an idea from Amy. Geo and Torus had managed to get a sample of the glue, and Amy had instructed the chemistry department to reproduce the mushroom-bugs' alkaline secretions for future defensive purposes."

"Great. Not wanting to hurry you or anything but, hurry up!"

The chemical has now been produced."

"So," replied Hogart, slightly panicked. "If we survive the crash, we can fight them off with water pistols?"

Spiney remained calm. "With your permission I would like to filter it through the nanite security systems, and out onto the surface of the Stellar Flash."

Hogart's mouth opened in surprise, instantly working out what Spiney had in mind. "Do it." He immediately turned to his security officer. "Puppy. Help Spiney."

"Yes, sir!"

Puppy quickly activated the security protocols for the nanite ship surface and rerouted the commands to Spiney's station. Spiney transmitted the liquid to the nanite distribution system, activating the program that would send the liquid along various microshafts to the surface of the Stellar Flash.

Down the back corridor from the Center and towards the edge of the Stellar Flash, a room lit up. Thousands of microbots, nanites and other tiny metallic systems went to work, straightening cables and sending liquid upward and downward, through the thick hull.

Outside the ship, hundreds of black and brown mushroom-bugs twitched their colored antennae as the binary stars shone behind them, and wisps of gas rushed past them. Below, the reddish-purple ground was slowly getting closer, conical buildings mere specks, but steadily getting larger.

"Alright, explain," said Heartness to no one in particular.

"The mushbugs are stuck to the outside using their own secretions, ma'am," said Spiney. "Their telekinesis is not strong enough. They have two main secretions. One that sticks and one that releases. Well, this plan is going to cover the Stellar Flash in the release liquid."

"That's brilliant!" said Heartness.

"Right!" Hogart looked quite happy at this development. "AI. As soon as the mushbugs start sliding off, set course for the next planet. Maximum speed."

"Confirmed," said the AI.

Suddenly, one of the mushbugs fell off the side, its antennae flicking widely as it flew away in the wind. The other mushbugs looked agitated, their antennae twitching at this unexpected situation. Then, almost as one, they pointed their antennae down to the surface of the craft, as though realizing something was wrong.

Seconds later, having lost a grip on the situation, all the mushbugs flew off the falling ship and were carried away by the air currents and re-entry slipstream.

Heartness looked amazed at the surround screen as the mushbugs flew off the outside of the ship, falling away from them.

"Control returned," said the AI. "Setting most

logical course."

"Spiney, that was an amazing solution. Thank you very much," said Hogart. "Just don't leave it too late next time."

"I'm very impressed," said Heartness. "Are you sure you wouldn't want to spend some time on X-1a as my PA?"

"There is no need for your complimentary behavior," said Spiney. "However, it is welcome."

"Captain?" called Cuddly. "I thought you wanted to go to another planet. We do not seem to be going in the right direction."

Hogart saw the screens and the rapidly approaching ground.

They hadn't changed course.

"AI. What is going on? I thought I told you to go to the next planet."

"Yes, sir."

"Why are we heading towards the surface of this one?"

"There is no planet there, sir."

"AI, yes there is. The brown and purple one. We can see it. You're driving us straight towards it." Hogart's voice had an edge of fear to it.

"Logical course set," said the AI. "Do you wish to choose a different location?"

Hogart knew there was no time. He gripped the stand as the side of a massive conical building on a collision course filled the screen.

Chapter 16
Released

Hogart screwed his eyes tightly shut as the Stellar Flash fell towards the top of the building…

…and passed through.

When he felt nothing, he opened his eyes to see Heartness staring at him.

She slapped his face.

"Get a *#!%^*> pilot!" she yelled.

Hogart fell back in shock as frequency-shifted rooms, tunnels, caves, underground rivers, then liquid carbon dioxide and magma rushed through him.

The AI had taken the most logical course. Frequency shift the ship to be slightly outside the existence of the planet so that they could simply fall through it to the other side.

Amazing.

But now his face hurt.

"Ow! Ma'am. I don't believe your actions are suitable for the position of Admiral."

"Oh, *#!% my admiral position. You're obviously an incompetent buffoon. I have no idea why Patel recommended you for this mission."

Suddenly angrier than he'd been for a while, Hogart stomped forward and thrust his face directly into Heartness'. "Ma'am. With all due respect, you can go back to your plushy little desk job while the real captains are out here completing their missions, risking their lives and limbs. I'm grateful you turned up when you did but, if you're not willing to let me make some changes, then I politely request you to GET THE *#!% OFF MY SHIP. Of course, if it's just your day of the month, I politely request you get your *#!%^*> emotions under *#!%^*> control!"

Heartness stepped back, her mouth open in shock. She raised her hand as though she was going to hit him again, then stopped.

Cuddly saw his chance and quickly inched his way, nervously, between them.

Captain Hogart was gasping for breath, angry, feeling betrayed, his left cheek smarting and turning red. Cuddly turned to him first.

"Captain, you may not have realized it, but we have all been affected by the binary suns. We have never seen Captain, sorry, Admiral Heartness ever hit someone, or even display these strong emotions before. We don't know you but we're sure you wouldn't be insulting an admiral if you were yourself either. I believe your natural human stubbornness has increased."

He turned to the admiral. "Ma'am, with all due respect, if you have a problem with the new command of this ship, I respectively ask you to take it through the relevant channels, or discuss this in private. This is not a forum for airing grievances. All the crew here will make allowances for the disruptive reality we are in now, but if you could please be more professional. I believe your natural human annoyance has increased."

Heartness shook, suddenly realizing what she had done. She looked confused. She reached out to Cuddly who inched away a little, so she pulled her hand back. "It's alright Cuddly. I think I've got it."

She took a deep breath, awkwardly walked around Cuddly and went over to Hogart who stood staring at her, simmering. She briefly looked at the other crew members. They were all watching her, wondering what this strange human would do next.

Tears, unbidden, came to her eyes, as her annoyance quickly turned to guilt. She touched a finger to her cheek in surprise as she felt one drip from her lashes.

A particularly dense level of lava began rising through the room, the reddish movement making the Center look almost demonic.

Slowly she walked around Hogart's station and went over to him. This time, she carefully placed her hand on his cheek, tears streaming down her face. "Oh Jonathan, I'm so, so sorry. It feels like I'm menopausal or overtired, or something. I don't know what affect the suns are having on me, but I'm really not myself. I should never have hit you. Can you forgive me?"

She stepped back to give him some space and held out her arms, biting her lip, looking for a hug.

Hogart's heart melted when he saw his friend crying, broken and vulnerable. He nodded dumbly, and Heartness came over to him and hugged him, held him tight, her arms rubbing his back, whispering 'I'm sorry, I'm sorry' in his ear, then stroking his face, stroking his neck, stroking his…

Moments later they were kissing passionately as the level of frequency shifted magma rose and completely blurred out all light in the Stellar Flash.

Puppy made a tsk tsk sound. "Humans!" his translator said. The other aliens couldn't help but agree with him.

It would be another half an hour before the Stellar Flash made it to the other side and began its course towards the first planet.

Storyteller's note: Information regarding this period of time during the mission could not be retrieved from any crew member. Suspect temporal anomaly.

Chapter 17
The Three Bodies Problem

"Well, here we are," said Heartness.

The room was quite nondescript. Barely fifty square meters with a cupboard at the back and three flat sheets of blue materials on separate shelves. Next to this was a complicated looking machine with pipes of liquid connected to a horizontal glass tube.

"We've never been here before," said Hogart, looking around distastefully.

"You've never been here before. This is where the Storytellers are stored." Heartness pointed at the three sheets on the shelves.

Hogart raised an eyebrow. He'd known about them, but this was the first time he'd had the chance to see any of them. Even so, his eyes were drawn to the middle shelf where the most interesting looking one seemed to lay.

The Storytellers were a race of people from the upper levels of Frequency Zero that could flit in between Zero and One quite easily. They were able to remember their experiences in Frequency One and bring memories of them back to Frequency Zero. Most aliens were only able to bring back symbolic representations of their memories, which tended to be incomplete or suffer from perception filtering.

All ships that shifted between Frequencies required a Storyteller to keep a record. Unfortunately, Jorjarar had been killed by the Queen and so, the ship no longer had any way to bring the records back.

"Do we really need one? This mission hasn't been going that well, and I'd really like to forget it," said Hogart.

"Captain Hogart, you know this is law. And, besides, if nothing was recorded, how would you explain the deaths of your three crew members to their families? Without a record, you might not just be legally responsible, you might be tried for their murder personally."

"I'm sorry that they died, but I still have a problem with the Storyteller monitoring all our thoughts."

They approached the cupboard and looked at the three blue sheets lying on the shelves. Each one had a raised shape that looked like an alien.

"You're kidding me," said Hogart. "Are they in some kind of suspended animation?"

"They're like tardigrades. You can remove all their moisture and store them, then just bring them out when they're needed. Many of them have lived for hundreds of thousands of years, so being flat for a few of them doesn't affect them at all."

Hogart looked at the three bodies on the shelves and wondered what to do. "Any particular order?"

"If you start saying eenie meenie I'm going to be very upset," said Heartness.

Hogart had been about to bring his fingers out but thought better of it.

"But we've already lost over half of the mission," said Hogart. "Will the Storyteller be able to figure out what has already happened from our memories?"

"In this rare situation, when you lose a Storyteller, the new one will fill in the gaps from the existing records and any memories it can get, but it may not be that accurate in getting every person's observations. Don't forget it won't just be monitoring the crew in the Center, it will be monitoring all of the crew. It has no idea who will be involved in the final story, so it needs to be aware of every member, then make a decision about what information is relevant when it gets back to Frequency Zero. We might not end up with all of the crew's views."

Hogart looked closely at the outlines. In this situation, he'd probably want to get the biggest one, just in case the Queen somehow tried to attack again. That looked to be number two, a handsome, hairy four-armed, two-legged creature with a long powerful snout that looked a bit like an Earth bear. "Greg," said Hogart, reading the tag. "Did you name these?"

"I think the Storytellers deliberately gave themselves names that we might like."

Hogart looked at the other names. Geemoneel and Sesheenleoo. Well, at least none of them were called Solo. He liked the name of Greg the most. It seemed to represent a strong Storyteller name. "Alright. I think Greg is the best choice. Let's get him into the system."

Hogart pulled up the half-tube glass covering, then grabbed the thin blue block of 'Greg' and put him carefully inside. Then he pulled the lid down, making sure it was completely sealed.

"I was just thinking," he said. "He's got four powerful arms, and by the look of it, four compelling eyes. Two on the front and two on the back giving him excellent all-round vision – better than most aliens. Won't the fact that he's used to having four arms and seeing 360 degrees cause the record to be a bit strange?"

"What do you mean?"

"Well, I just think if we're trying to create records for human beings, we need to get a humanoid to represent the story here. Otherwise, we'll get pretty alien concepts creeping into the storyline." Hogart absently rubbed his sides, wishing he had four arms like the creature in front of him. He couldn't imagine how he could have survived so long with just two.

Heartness laughed. "Oh, we have a human editor at the other end that should catch most of these. As many people reading the stories are going to have an interest in science fiction too, the editor's job also includes replacing many of the Storyteller's alien jokes with human references to past SF hits. Usually something obscure from the 21st century so that it doesn't really interrupt the flow of the conversation or act as a red herring for the story but can cause a devout SF fan to groan."

"Fantastic," said Hogart, reaching over and turning on the activation button. "Rehydrate, rehydrate."

The tubes filled with multiple liquids of many colors, and the block immediately began to inflate, the creature's head, torso, arms and legs popping up and getting larger. Then Hogart realized that there wasn't any block anymore as the edges were absorbed into the recreation of the creature. Soon there was just a hairy, blue, four-armed bear-like Greg inside the tube.

A graph on the side of the capsule began to beep with life signs, and Greg's eyes flickered awake.

"Well," said Hogart. "It looks like my privacy is over."

Greg set to work, connecting his mind to the Stellar Flash interface and recovering some of the lost materials from Jorjarar's records. Much of Jorjarar's records were, unfortunately, not up to Greg's standards and had to have extensive rewrites to be more accurate. Greg was surprised to find that in the first draft, most of the aliens had overlarge mammary glands. Even the males. He was happy to have been able to fix some of that storyline.

The crew had shifted the Storyteller's area to a new place, far away from the Quarantine bay, at Greg's request. They were very happy to get him anything he wanted.

Greg was very concerned that his predecessor had met an untimely death but was very happy with the care and interest that all the crew took in him. When he walked to his recording room, many of the aliens on board greeted him, told him how honored they were to give him their memories for his records, and how they looked forward to continuing to work with him in the future.

Both Heartness and Hogart bowed to Greg as he set up, then left him to enjoy the comforts of his Storytelling area as only someone as sophisticated and handsome as Greg could.

"I guess, if there is a section about Greg in the records, it'll be positive and glowing?" asked Hogart.

"Oh, no. I'm sure the Storytellers are incredibly unbiased. They need to see all sides, so anything that Greg writes will be absolutely accurate."

"That's good to hear. He seems very trustworthy," said Hogart.

"Oh, he is," agreed Heartness.

The Stellar Flash continued on its way to its next destination where they hoped to find more of the strangely armless mushbugs.

Chapter 18
Evolution

The Stellar Flash turned slightly and settled into orbit around the blue and brown planet. Thicker cloud cover obscured much of the surface, but what they could see suggested a similar amount of land to the previous planet they'd visited. Though, it wasn't as brown and purple as the other ones.

"Zooming now," said Amy.

The spherical screen zoomed its view down to one of the land masses, and both Hogart and Heartness gasped at what it returned. Thousands of brown and black mushbugs with wings and legs flying about huge conical multiple-door mounds that stretched at least a kilometer into the sky.

This planet had more water than the last, the sky was blue and the oxygen levels were higher. Some of the structures looking artistic, some looked functional, but all were clean and did not look like there was anything remotely polluting about them.

"OMG! It's a mushbug utopia," said Hogart.

Heartness nodded. "Well, this is more like it. Wish our drones had been able to translate this information to our frequency."

"So, the Queen is from a less developed nation, still bent on war. This one has passed that," said Hogart.

As the planet turned beneath them, they quickly viewed more of the civilization, from floating structures on the water, to energy conversion systems to low orbital elevators.

"Captain," said Cuddly. "I'm receiving a message. They have detected our presence and would like to make contact."

Hogart grinned. "Well, let's make contact!" he said.

Hogart had decided that, this time, the meeting should take place on their ship. He didn't want a repeat of what had happened last time he met the mushbugs. A brief flashback of Cuddly spraying him caused him to shudder. Definitely not.

With the Queen's pieces secure, everyone across the ship had packed away their nanite suits and were watching the unfolding first contact meeting happen via their in-room terminals. If something was to go wrong with the meeting, they were ready to activate their suits again.

The Center crew decided to wait in hangar one and greet their guests when they arrived. From this vantage point they could see just a sliver of the planet, and a tiny round speck leaving orbit and getting larger.

Moments later, a large oval ship, almost mushbug-shaped, with no obvious propulsion, floated through the force field and landed, extending six landing struts. The front of the ship dissolved, little hexagonal pieces folding back, and several mushbugs floated out.

As they took up positions in a row along the outside of the craft, Hogart noted some interesting details.

These mushbugs looked slightly different to the ones they'd encountered before. Not only were their eyes bigger and their stomachs ridgeless, featuring six legs like the Queen, there were definite male and female attributes. The males seemed to be slightly larger with spikes on their claws, while the females seemed to be slightly longer. Both of these new types of mushbugs had long tails, too.

The wings were a noticeable difference, however, but these were kept under their shell casings. They looked more like fins than wings, and Hogart suspected they were only used for guidance.

Telekinetic ability seemed to have molded the entire civilization.

"They look a bit like a cross between horseshoe crabs and trilobites," whispered Hogart, his antennae on silent.

"But are more plant than animal," said Amy, hers also on silent, waiting for the first mushbug to speak.

All the crew wore their nanite suits, and this time they'd all grown antennae to communicate.

"Admiral, I believe you should do the honors." Hogart indicated for Heartness to step forward.

"Oh, no. I'm just a passenger. It's your ship now."

"I was afraid you'd say that." He stepped over to be directly in front of the mushbugs and said a prepared speech for these occasions, glad that he could finally use it. "Though minds and body forms may be different, it is through the heart that we are one." His antennae scratched then twisted with the sentences.

The leader mushbug seemed to react positively, its antennae replying that it was a great honor to meet them, though Hogart was worried he might be anthropomorphizing again.

But he was sure there were some similarities across the alien cultures. After all, if they didn't attack, then you could assume that they were friendly, right?

Feeling safer in this knowledge, though also slightly uncomfortable considering it was only a few hours ago that the Queen had tried to dismember him in that very room, Hogart led the mushbugs out of the hangar. They headed into the wide corridors that led to a more comfortable meeting room. The rest of his crew followed.

The meeting room had been decorated with brown and white wall paneling, the pattern broken by strips of black wood, with lots of soft mats, Japanese style. With the mushbugs preferring their legs to be folded under them when not moving, Hogart thought this was probably the best way to have a meeting, though the five heavy antennae on his back meant leaning forward cross-legged was probably going to require a few days rest to recover.

The darker brown-colored mushbug began speaking. "You may address me as Scart," it said. "I believe you must record our meeting, and names will make things easier for you."

"Thank you, Scart," said Hogart, nodding. "You may address me as Jonathan."

"We will not, but we understand the exchange. It is not our culture to have names."

"Well, Scart, how do you tell each other apart?"

"We are all parts of the whole."

"So, you have a Queen too?"

At this Scart quickly flicked his antennae at his companions who replied back, theirs flicking ominously fast.

"You visited the lower planet," the main mushbug stated. "We monitored your arrival and departure."

Hogart raised his eyes at this. The frequency they'd chosen really didn't work here.

"We recorded a slight mass shift which suggested a large amount of matter had left the planet. We assumed a queen was seeding, or perhaps another immigration attempt. What can you tell us about that?"

Hogart looked embarrassed. "We attempted to make first contact with the Queen on that planet during her splitting period and were jailed, then blackmailed. The Queen wanted our technology."

"Ah," said Scart. "So, you captured her?"

"Err, not exactly. She broke apart when she hit our ship. We collected all her pieces and she put herself together, killed three of my crew, then we found a way to pull her apart again before she killed anyone else."

"Killed?" asked Scart. It looked like he needed more information on this matter. Had they laws regarding queens killing aliens? He conferred with his companions further, then turned to Hogart. "You can die?"

Hogart looked surprised. "Well, yes. We only have one life, and then we die when we either have a severe accident or get too old."

Scart seemed to look concerned. "You are inferior. We don't want to be infected by your death disease."

"What?"

"Thank you for this meeting. We must go. Please escort us back to our ship."

The mushbugs began to get up and Heartness interrupted, her suit making the scratching attention sound. "Excuse me. But we know consciousness is eternal. We shift from body to body. As each body wears out we go into another frequency in another form for a time, then choose a new body and grow up again."

The mushbugs saw Heartness' message but continued leaving. "This is unacceptable. If you die, you cannot remember anything. Society cannot grow. You will end up making the same mistakes again and again. You are stuck in repeating cycles. We only move forward, never back."

Heartness looked at Hogart disappointedly as the aliens left. The other crew members remained silent. There was nothing they could do.

It seemed that the immortals were mortalists.

Hogart frowned. There was something... He quickly got up, ignoring the pain in his legs from sitting cross-legged, and ran after the mushbugs. "Wait, one more question, why do you not help the lower planet? You could bring them your advancements, your technology. Help them to mature."

"They are stuck in their cycle of breeding. Until they remove the Queen and choose advancement over hierarchical power structures, they are under quarantine."

"But, that's what our plan is. We are offering you membership in a multidimensional organization that contain trillions of mortal and immortal races working together. If we decide that your society is not yet developed enough, we will quarantine your star system from the rest of the universe."

Scart stopped moving, its antennae giving strange jerking movements. The other mushbugs also gave the same movement. It wasn't translatable. Were they laughing?

They turned and headed to the hangar, entered their ship and headed back into space without another flick.

Hogart watched them go.

First Contact negotiations in this system were a lot harder than he thought.

Hogart and Heartness were in the Center looking glum. They should just take the Queen back to her world and leave.

"We are being contacted again, Captain," said Cuddly.

"Put it through," said Hogart, slightly hopeful.

Scart's image filled one of the screens, and his antennae flicked quickly.

"We apologize for our rudeness. We were in shock that we may have contracted your death disease. Fortunately, our doctors have cleared us and confirm that it isn't something we can catch. Our analysis indicates you are all simply replicated DNA strands, and as you're all just copies within copies, you're bound to break down eventually."

The translator struggled to keep up with the complicated twisting of the mushbug's antennae.

"However, we should follow the protocol that we have absorbed from your ship to show respect for your organization. We honorably decline your invitation to join your group. We are quite happy on our little world, and have chosen a time of peace, contemplation and exclusion as we are due for metamorphosis. Alien contact has no use for us at this time. Please save your technology and resources for someone more suitable for your endeavor."

The image clicked off before anyone had a chance to say a word.

Hogart looked stunned. "Well, that's that, then!" he said.

"I'm not so sure," said Heartness. "I wonder what their metamorphosis is. Perhaps they'll be different after they go through that process."

"So, we might have First Contact with them in the near future."

Hogart stared at the blue and white world on his right, slowly turning, displaying the mushbug utopia. What could their metamorphosis be? Were they shifting to fourth density? Perhaps becoming less corporeal?

Geo interrupted his thoughts. "Captain. The drones have returned from the binaries and the results are, well, I think you'll need to see my astrophysicist's interpretation of the data."

Hogart made his way over to Geo's screen and placed his hand on it. If Geo wanted him to see this privately, it must be something particularly disturbing.

He activated his mind view system and watched as the information scrolled across it. He gasped in alarm, and gripped Geo's stand to stop from falling over.

He took a breath and gathered himself, turning to the others. "Everyone needs to know about this." He transmitted the information to the surround screen.

"Oh my God," said Heartness, covering her mouth.

"Now what do we do?" returned Hogart, steadying himself.

Chapter 19
The One is All and the All are One

The Stellar Flash was speedily moving towards one of the suns of the system, which was further away around the elliptic. Its route had been carefully calculated to avoid any contact with any other space debris, asteroids, comets and, more particularly, dormant queen mushbugs.

While that would usually be easy to do with billions of kilometers between them, the fact that queens had the propensity for seeding by launching themselves into space, meant colliding with a dormant queen that had been floating for thousands of years was a real possibility. Not to mention the occasional cloud of dormant dark mushbugs.

There was one central sun, with the other smaller sun orbiting it along with all the other planets. Even though the smaller sun was close, it had been lucky enough to remain in orbit, rather than be pulled into the mass of the main star. It was still close enough, however, to prevent any other planets from orbiting between them.

Just as well, thought Hogart. Any planet there would just be a lump of molten rock.

The ship had now reached about 3000 kilometers distance from the smaller sun and was monitoring it.

"How's everyone holding up?" asked Hogart. He was starting to feel stubborn again, and he could see that Heartness had been banging her station a few times, when it took a few more seconds than usual to refresh. He wondered how being this close to the binary suns was likely to affect the other crew members.

Almost as if reading his mind, Amy said "Captain, I need you in my quarters, now!" Her shape wasn't stable, and she was flicking out tendrils, trying to reach the other aliens but stopping herself. "You too, Admiral. I don't think I can handle this."

"Amy, take a break and, um, take the AI pumice stone with you. Set for tangibility." The last thing Hogart wanted was to suddenly have Amy on the Center floor. What would Heartness think?

Amy immediately slurped herself off the console and squelched, rolled and otherwise slid out the Center door and down the corridor, with the AI floating behind.

Hogart was also starting to feel strange, but in a different way this time. He recognized the headache. Rejection of his mind view implant. But he had the patches on. His body shouldn't be rejecting it now. He shook his head. As soon as it started to clear, he felt his fear of stars returning. He clenched his fists and gritted his teeth. He had to focus.

Then he smashed his fist on his station to refocus. The other aliens looked at him. "Oh, just trying to, um, get this station to work properly."

He was thankful that Amy had taken the AI stone with her, otherwise it would probably have said something like…

"Your station is operating normally, Captain Hogart," echoed the AI's voice.

"Oh, very meta. Thank you, AI." He groaned. He

decided he needed to distract everyone and, hopefully, distract himself.

"Alright team…," then it struck him. One of the station areas was empty. "Where's Torus?"

Heartness pointed at the floor where minor static flickers sparked and threaded towards the door. "The Stellar Flash EM field is being overloaded by the binary suns' fields. Torus can't hold himself together."

Hogart looked at the other crew members. Puppy was looking like he was going to faint, swaying on his twelve legs. Cuddly had gone to the toilet again but it had been his second time in only half an hour. Only Geo and Spiney seemed to be surviving.

"Sir," began Spiney. "I think my breeding cycle has been activated. I don't know why."

"But if you spray here, we'll all start growing your babies inside our lungs!" said Heartness, slightly annoyed.

"I am aware of this. Permission to confine myself to quarters."

"Absolutely, Spiney," said Hogart. "Please do what you have to do! And quickly!"

Spiney quickly shuffled out of the Center and through the door.

"Anyone else?"

A clacking could be heard from Puppy. He couldn't speak, and his tongue was inside his mouth for once. He'd also changed color, not a vibrant green. More like a sickly yellow. Hogart simply indicated the door nearest him, and Puppy clacked and stumbled towards it, exiting quickly.

Hogart had no idea how the stars would have affected Puppy, but with his great size, anything was possible.

Heartness was rubbing her red face with a handkerchief. "How long will we have to remain here, Jon? I think I'm getting hot flushes."

Hogart pointed at Cuddly who had just returned from another toilet break. "He's trying to find a language. If we can communicate with it, we might be able to have a successful mission, after all."

The orbs had brought back some incredibly startling news. While one returned with perfectly normal spectrographic results for the main star, the second one had had everyone struggling to breathe. Somehow the smaller star was made up of lots of pieces of something stuck together.

It was entirely possible the secondary star was completely made up of billions of generations of mushbugs.

Hogart looked at the zoomed screen showing the corona of the smaller star. Except that he knew it wasn't really a corona. It was some kind of protective force field that behaved exactly like one. In fact, the hot body was so similar to a star that they had had no way of knowing from spectrographical reports. Only when the orb brought back visual images had they been able to know for sure.

As they got closer, the second star almost blanked out the front of the view panel, its light turning everything white-orange, even with the filters on their lowest setting. Hogart involuntarily covered his eyes.

Being this close to a star filled him with dread. If it wasn't for the fact that the ship could withstand temperatures of even a blue star, he would have quite easily quit his post and gone back to running an entertainment company on Earth. Of course, his dream had always been to get into space, even creating endless dream shows and mind view series on the subject in his spare time, and he was definitely very happy to be finally in command of his own ship. Even so, with that horrifying burning ball of plasma so close, those flickers of black death, swirls of pain, spouts of fiery damnation, and the feeling he was staring into the pit of hell itself, he was tempted to run here and now.

The last thing he wanted was anyone to think he was heliophobic.

"Captain, I am detecting an elevated heart rate, increased perspiration, and a spike in adrenaline in your biological projection," stated Geo. "Are you being affected by the star in a new way?"

"It's okay, Geo," said Heartness. "I'm sure the Captain is just feeling a bit scared at being so close."

"Scared?" said Hogart quickly, slightly indignantly. He knew Heartness was deliberately teasing him to distract him. He should play along to ease her mind a little. He was sure he had got over his heliophobia when he was a child. He shouldn't feel this fearful as an adult. "Never. It's not so scary this close up, is it! And, I know we have nothing to worry about."

Heartness winked at him and subtly made a soft fist with her hand a couple of times. Hogart looked down at his own. His fists were clenched so hard the knuckles were white. He quickly released them and winked back at her. She didn't need a computer to tell her how stressed he was.

"Well, team. We're here. What can you tell me?"

"The corona seems to be generated on the outside, rather than coming from within," said Geo. "Outside, it is a common star, but just beneath the surface, it is not. I believe this energy is being generated from the spin of the shell structure within the star's EM field. I have many statistics. Shall I read them out to you?"

"No, it's alright Geo. Thanks. Cuddly, you're sure this star is sentient?"

"Mushbug pieces arranged in a sphere shape billions of kilometers in diameter, with no breaks or mismatch of any kind? Yes."

Hogart didn't know if Cuddly's sarcasm was intentional or not. "How do we make contact?"

Cuddly zoomed the cameras into a section of the star. Soon, the surround screen was completely enveloped in swirling, broiling sunspots and fiery gas plumes. The image was thousands of kilometers away, yet Hogart seemed to feel the heat. He was sure his skin was starting to burn. His perspiration increased.

The image zoomed further, breaking through clouds of gas to focus directly on a blurred area beneath the surface. A faint outline could be seen through the wavering image. Cuddly enhanced the image. A giant hexagon.

"You're kidding me," said Hogart, suddenly realizing exactly what Cuddly had in mind. "No, no, no."

He lifted his hands up in a stop gesture and began backing away from his station before stopping himself. Sweat beaded on his temple and began running down his face. *I can't do this. I can't do this.*

"The field is only 7,000 degrees Celsius," said Cuddly. "The ship can withstand that. But the field would block any kind of signal we try to get to it. We need to touch the star. The only way to do that is to land."

"I can't risk 300 people! I need something more

definite." Hogart's voice sounded higher than usual.

"Captain." Heartness turned to him, not wanting to take command, wanting to give him the confidence, but knowing that Hogart was on the borderline of a panic attack. She had to relax him somehow. "We have several options, but only one is going to work. You could send a probe, but they may not notice it. You could send an android in the scout craft, but they may not identify it. We could shift into a slightly different frequency where the heat won't affect us, but we would still need to shift back to make contact. At the end of the day, this is your mission. Imagine it. You would be the first captain in human history to land his ship on a star!"

"Well, it's not really a star," said Hogart, thinking. But everyone else would still think it was. It would look great on his resume. And the stories he could tell girls at the bar...

Hogart put on a grin, trying to focus on the more positive aspects. "Well, Admiral. You've persuaded me." He said, lightly. Outwardly he looked composed and confident and was no longer sweating. Inwardly, he shuddered at the thought, swallowed, then turned to speak with the AI, then remembered the rock had disappeared. He looked around the ship, slightly confused. *Where do you look when there is no AI avatar to look at?* He looked at the hexagon on the front screen, its shape warping under the intense heat and plasma plumes.

"AI, plot a course to land on that hexagon."

The yellow hexagon seemed to fill the screen as the AI replied. "Confirmed."

There was a slight hum as their EM drive engaged, and the ship quickly flitted the last few thousand kilometers through two flares, and slowly settled down onto the hexagon-shaped pseudo landing pad. As the Stellar Flash settled, Hogart saw, disturbingly, the billions of hexagons stretching out under the fiery surface, an entire star made up of them.

Without warning, the hexagonal platform dissolved into gas, and the Stellar Flash plummeted through the surface.

Heartness had been given the pilot's station, and she had tried to avoid even looking at it, let alone using it. Having recently argued with Hogart about the lack of a pilot, the last thing she wanted to do was be one. But, as she wasn't officially there, and she wasn't entirely comfortable about throwing her rank around, the pilot station was hers.

When the ship fell through the gaseous opening, she grabbed the station for support, and as though sensing her danger, her little shuttle craft, the Stellar Breeze, communicated with her through the console.

"What?" she said in surprise. Then she looked about to see if the crew had heard the voice.

From their slow movements Heartness knew something had happened to everyone else except her. Perhaps her ship had sped her timestream up.

"Consciousness is faster," said a voice in her head. Heartness looked at the image on the surround screen. They had slowed in their fall, almost frozen in time. Only she was unaffected. Why?

"Paradox here. Paradox being created. Paradox already destroyed," said the voice. "You were there at the beginning."

"What can I do?" Heartness slapped at the console, trying to get more information without success. "Can

Hogart fix it?"

"Torus will be the one. You must help him."

Briefly Heartness thought how annoyed Hogart was going to feel when he found out he wasn't going to be the one to save them. Still, he couldn't expect every mission to be completed by him.

"How?"

"EM field boost to recombine him. Be the conduit between myself and the Older."

The Older? The Stellar Flash?

Heartness placed her hands on the white pilot's panel and this time images began rushing through her mind. This station used to belong to Leafy, Heartness' previous pilot. Earth had found the Stellar Flash consciousness responded better to female plant-based lifeforms. Earth hadn't been comfortable with that but the type of brain frequency required meant no human pilot could completely merge with it. But her little ship said she could. Perhaps all those hours she'd spent on board had changed her to be closer to the Stellar Flash's frequency. And now she had her own ship to help her complete the connection.

What would it be like? How would she know?

Heartness blinked, and the entire Center disappeared. She was floating in space, with a wall of fiery yellow hexagons as far as her eyes could see. She immediately began to panic as she wasn't wearing a nanite, force or standard space suit. How could she survive? Was there an atmosphere?

Then she noticed that she couldn't hear her own breath or heartbeat. She wasn't physically in space.

She was the Stellar Flash.

She moved her head and the Stellar Flash shifted slightly in the liquid. She bent forward and she could feel the ship redesigning itself, becoming thicker in the middle. She stopped.

What was she doing? She had to save Torus. How? Command it?

"Consciousness of Stellar Flash. Strengthen the EM field around the ship so that Torus can recombine."

Nothing happened.

"Stellar Flash, how do I use the power of the Stellar Breeze to increase the EM field barrier?"

Nothing

"Stellar Breeze? Stellar Flash isn't responding."

"You are Stellar Flash."

Heartness sighed. Great. Of course she was.

But she'd forgotten what the Stellar Flash could do. Did she cough? No, that would release the waste disposal. What if she clenched a fist?

She felt herself move forward faster. Opening her fist slowed her down. She knew in the real world her body wasn't actually doing that - these were the mental responses that were needed for particular functions.

"This is crazy. Help me!"

"Consciousness is not a doing. Not masculine energy. Consciousness is allowing. Female energy. Allow it to happen. I will help. Once reformed, Torus will not need the field again inside."

Heartness stopped looking for a control or command, and simply relaxed, imagining Torus recombining. Imagining the field around the ship strengthening.

Then she felt it. The hairs were rising on the back of her arms. The command and the result were linked. She knew how to do it after she had done it.

A stabilizing energy rushed over the ship. Energy

poured from the Stellar Breeze, combining with the field and strengthening it.

Her face felt warmer as though confirming the new command, and then the Center appeared around her again.

Still connected to the pilot's station she could sense the fields within the room. A fluctuating energy wave was becoming stable, changing its configuration.

Torus was coming back together.

With a flash, Torus recombined next to his station as though nothing had happened. Heartness felt the strengthened EM field return to normal, and Torus flickered slightly as though adjusting to the new environment.

He was safe. She felt a wave of appreciation from the two ships, and released her hand from the pilot's station.

And then, suddenly, everything was back to normal, so to speak.

Captain Hogart grabbed his console for support as the center of gravity suddenly changed again, an alarm sounded, and red lights began flashing. "Report!"

All the screens were showing shifting images of a yellow wall full of bright hexagons rushing past them. It stretched away from them as far as the eye could see. Even though the ship was now falling, Hogart could see that their hole had already sealed over, the gas reverting back to solid matter. They were trapped inside.

"AI, stabilize the ship!"

"In progress," said the AI.

Hogart continued gripping his station but could feel the ship starting to become more controllable. "The star is hollow. I assume whatever we need to meet is near the center. Set a heading, and move slowly in, but don't get too close."

"Captain, I'm not sure that's wise," said Heartness, still reeling from her recent experience. She had to let time run its course until Torus could do whatever he had to do.

"Now who's being pessimistic!" He turned back to the block. "AI. Search for a safe orbit around the gravitational well."

"Confirmed."

Heartness looked appreciatively. "I'm glad you don't actually want to go to the center. I'm pretty sure that even the Stellar Flash wouldn't be able to withstand that much gravity."

"Well, now that we know this is an entire world disguised as a star, I'm guessing there really isn't anything at the center besides warped space. In any case, I'm not big on time dilation either."

"Analysis suggests, based on human theoretical constructs, that this may be a reverse Dyson sphere," said Geo.

"They built the sphere inside a star?" asked Hogart incredulously. "How is that even possible?"

Just then the ship stabilized and the images on the screen settled down. Hogart watched billions more hexagons speed past. "I had no idea when I woke up today that I'd end up inside a star that had been created by a Doctor Who fan."

"You're not still watching that series, are you?" said Heartness, sounding pleased to have any kind of distraction.

"Celebrating 170 years this year!" said Hogart, "Though I wasn't sure I'd keep watching when the main character turned into a genderless energy being last year."

As the ship straightened, the screens revealed a tiny light that shone brightly in the center, millions of kilometers away. Even though the sphere was lit from outside and within, everything seemed washed out and unclear.

"So, there is something at the center," said Heartness.

"Captain, I think there are some statistics you really need to know," said Geo.

"Shoot!"

Geo stopped and looked at the Captain. "At what?"

"Sorry, that didn't translate well. Tell me please, Geo."

"I'm detecting a thick, high pressure atmosphere. Oxygen, nitrogen, hydrogen, methane and a number of other elements."

"Are there living things here? A civilization?"

Just then, Puppy and Amy reentered the Center, with the AI's rock avatar floating behind.

A message also came from Spiney saying that, for safety, he should remain in his cabin. Hogart agreed.

Hogart suddenly realized that he was feeling a lot better, too. His mind view system wasn't fighting to get out of his head. "I guess we're beyond the field that's been affecting everyone in the star system!" he said. "Welcome back team. Glad to have you back."

His crew took their places. "I've been monitoring everything from my cabin," said Amy. "There is definitely life here. But probably not what you're expecting."

"Let me guess," said Hogart. "The hexagons are the life. The whole sphere is one huge orgy of merged creatures, and we're now inside it. It's going to want to make us part of it."

"Not exactly," said Amy. "Though it might have been like that millions of years ago. No, we are in a thin microbial soup. We are flying through a star-sized ball of bacteria. You could say we're diving through a metagenomicist's dream."

Hogart looked surprised. "Are you sure? Can bacteria just live and float in an atmosphere like this?"

"We can't tell with our sensors, and the image won't show it, but I believe the environment is so thick with the bacteria that it is almost like we are underwater."

"And they're all living and surviving with only the energy of the star outside and in to sustain them?"

"It's completely symbiotic, self-repairing and with a level of sophistication far in advance of any bacteriological symbiotic relationship ever heard of in this or any other frequency," said Amy. "It would be like taking the ship through your blood stream."

Hogart stared out at the screens in amazement. Was the bacteria now a completely sentient star-sized organism, or was the star the organism and the bacteria was keeping it alive? Or both?

"Back to you, Cuddly." Hogart pointed at his communications officer who had just returned from another toilet visit.

"We are not directly in contact with one of the hexagons, but we are now part of the star's biological soup," said Cuddly. "Knowing that this is just one giant mushbug means I can try sending a message alert. We should be able to communicate directly."

Just then a booming voice echoed around the Center and across the entire ship.

"Finality," it said. "End."

"That doesn't sound good," said Puppy.

"The One is the All and the All are one," said the voice.

"Cuddly, will it understand? We don't need to flick antennae at it?"

"It's an advanced creature living across a number of densities. Though, it might not yet be aware we're individuals."

There was silence as they thought about this, then the voice boomed again.

"We know you."

The voice seemed to echo into other voices. The echoes reverberated around the ship as though coming from ghosts.

"We know you. We know you. Know you. Know you."

Neither feminine nor masculine the voices seemed to have an ethereal, almost angelic quality.

"I am Captain Jonathan Hogart of the Interdimensional Coalition starship the Stellar Flash. I and my crew of three hundred sentient aliens from around the galaxy come in peace."

"Pieces, pieces. We feel your pieces. Make us complete."

Hogart turned to Spiney. "Pieces?"

"The creature may be detecting the Queen, sir."

"The Queen! Of course. I had forgotten all about her. If they need her we need to get her back to them quickly before they pull us apart. Can we flash her into the center of the bacteria? I guess we'll need to flash a bubble of air first so as not to cause a problem for them."

"Well," said Torus. "I am not so sure about that, sir. We need to confirm what the star is actually saying."

Hogart turned to the AI. "Let's get prepared, just in case. AI, release the Queen's pieces from quarantine. Make sure all her pieces are there, including the one stuck on the back of the flash band. When she recreates herself, hold her in this frequency until we're ready to release her. She's from this star system, she may even be able to help us."

"Confirmed."

In the quarantine area, the forcefields surrounding the vats of the Queen turned off. A robot made of cables and clips with two tweezer-like appendages entered and stomped over to one of the tables where Hogart's first flash sat. It carefully removed the final piece from the underside of it and placed it on the pile of other tiny hexagons, then took the band with it as it left the room. It watched through the window as the Queen's pieces began shifting and moving again, hexagons slowly clicking back into place.

In the Center, Hogart was pacing back and forth with way too much on his mind. Out there was a hyper-advanced pan-dimensional being with a consciousness made up of quadrillions to the nth pieces of mushbug. Was this where all the queens eventually ended up? Spiraling back to the center of the star system and being captured inside the star, or did the star just invite them in and they happily joined? But, if they were now inside a giant queen billions of kilometers in diameter, they were mere bugs in comparison, and really had no value to the voice. What could they possibly offer something so far advanced? How could they even have any commonality?

He sighed. He was futuring again rather than taking the opportunity in the 'now' moment. He should just do what he came to do. If it didn't work out, he'd work something else out. He'd come this far.

He went to his stand again. "Might as well get on with it." He rubbed his hands together and took a deep breath.

"Hello, out there," he said. "We want to invite you into the Interdimensional Coalition as a full member. We are a group of aliens from across multiple space, time, frequencies and realities that have a passion for discovering new consciousnesses like you."

"Remember, remember," the voice echoed. "We remember you, Captain Jonathan Hogart. You came to our world twice."

Hogart looked around at everyone. "Is this an adventure that I haven't had yet, or don't remember?"

"Adjusting," said the echoing voice. "Must use lower consciousness expression. Activating interface."

On the screen, before the star, a faint image of a mushbug appeared. But this was an even more advanced version. The mushbug's mass seemed to have shrunk, its six legs had shifted around its body, and it now stood upright, almost humanoid. Then, its wings expanded and it looked like a ghostly humanoid butterfly with five antennae. Its mouth opened but remained unmoving in the soup. It was an avatar to enable communication, but it didn't exist.

"First, we captured you and your crew members. We wanted your technology."

Hogart was surprised at this. The star had been monitoring them.

"Then you visited us again when we were more advanced. But we didn't want your contact. We were too proud. Too bigoted. And we were due for metamorphosis."

"Wait, we visited two of your worlds. Perhaps this is not translating correctly."

"There is only one world," said the voice, more softly.

"Err, no, sorry," said Hogart, not quite understanding. Did it mean that the entire system was linked in some way? The system was the world. "There are thirty worlds. Lots of your relatives on them."

"There is only one world," the voice repeated. "We know you from our history."

Hogart turned to his crew, his face a mixture of confusion, and then the hair began to rise on the back of his neck as the pieces began to fall into place.

All his crew looked at him. Even across the many alien cultures and species, he could tell they were all reaching the same conclusion as him.

Heartness was shaking her head in wonder. "No way."

"It is impossible," said Geo.

The worlds they had visited. They weren't other worlds in the star system, they were the same world, moving closer and closer to the center.

The entire star system of thirty planets and two stars was actually just one planet and one star across billions of years. The Stellar Flash had not only been travelling across space, they had been travelling across time as well. Somehow time had overlapped in space. The entire history of the star system had been happening for them all at once.

No wonder they hadn't been feeling themselves. The temporal anomalies had been bringing parts of their pasts and futures to them.

But how had this happened? Had the effect of the creation of the joined world itself at the end of time, somehow dissolved the timelines?

"There aren't thirty planets, are there?" asked Hogart. "There was only ever one, slowly moving closer to its star, to its eventual evolution. But the creation of that new sentience split the timelines! You're now fighting amongst each other, flying to your own future and past, creating a massive paradox in space / time."

"No paradox. Infinite pasts and futures. The result is the result. All paths lead here," said the voice. "But you are the anachronism. Your existence created us."

Hogart hit his head. "Of course. Without us appearing in your past, you couldn't have discovered frequency development so early."

"I guess it was our first appearance that started it," said Heartness. "I'm as much at fault as you."

"There is no point in apportioning blame at this time," said Geo. "We must continue our mission."

Suddenly the ship spun, and the crew gripped their stations to stop from falling over.

"What's happening?" yelled Hogart.

The image of the butterfly mushbug enlarged to monstrous proportions, then disappeared as the ship plummeted through it, being dragged forward at high speed.

"The Stellar Flash is being attracted towards the center."

"Activate flash drive. Get us out of here," said Hogart.

"Negative. Flash drive cannot operate in this environment," said the AI.

"But we're not..." Hogart groaned. "How long until we reach the center?"

"One hour," said the AI. "But gravitational forces closer to the core will begin pulling us apart in a few minutes."

Hogart placed his hands on his console and sent a ship wide red alert. "All crew, we are heading towards a strong gravitational point. Please return to your cabins and lie perpendicular to the expected event horizon." Then more quietly to himself "…as soon as we can work out which side the ship will be facing."

"AI, can you stabilize the spin?" asked Heartness.

"Gravitational and bacteriological currents are hampering stabilization, admiral," replied the AI. "Adjusting outer surface shape for more streamlined navigation."

As the triangular shape of the ship shook and turned, moving faster through the sphere of bacteria fluid, molecules shifted and changed, shaping the corners, building out fins and slightly flattening the sphere in the center.

A screeching metal sound shook the Center and Hogart looked up to see the ceiling shift and lower, the two pieces of the center column now not far apart.

"Streamlining complete," said the AI. The images on the screen stopped spinning and shuddering, and began to return to a slight blur, with a focus on the star in the middle. It was now much closer and had a flickering flame at the center.

Hogart lifted his hand to the console and felt his fingers being pulled towards the front screen. He placed his hands down quickly and sent another message. "All crew, activate nanite suits. Program for fluctuating gravity. At this stage, if you dislocate anything, I'm sorry but there's nothing we can do for now. We'll get to you as soon as possible."

He looked about his crew. The closer they got to the star in the middle, the more stretched they were going to feel. Amy had already collapsed across her console and was sliding across the floor, her translator warping as he watched. "Sorry, Captain. I can't help for now."

He looked across at Geo, but he had already passed out. Being ball shape, there wasn't any position he could be in without being affected by the pull of the gravity. His suit had put him into a coma to protect him.

Cuddly had already laid himself down perpendicular to the force of gravity.

There was a loud crash as Puppy could no longer support his own weight. Hogart hoped he hadn't broken anything.

He knew Heartness would be suffering as much as he was right now. He could feel every muscle stretching and many of his past sporting injuries had come back to haunt him. Just then he felt his jaw beginning to dislocate.

"Torus," Hogart groaned, trying to hold his head up, as the gravity began to pull harder. "You're in charge. Get us out of here, if you can."

With that, both Hogart and Heartness fell to the ground, unconscious.

Torus sensed the crew on the floor around him. What could he do?

The increasing gravity would simply kill them all and pull the ship apart. It was just a matter of a few more minutes.

He shifted to Cuddly's communications panel, connected with the broadcast systems and attempted communication with the creature's consciousness in the center of the star.

"You rejected them last time because they were not immortal like you," he projected. "If you do not stop pulling the ship to the center, they will all die."

The voice boomed chillingly. "Your DNA projections will die. But the bacteriological life within you will survive, long enough to become part of us."

"I am not bacteriological. There are other beings here that have no bacteria. What will you do with us?"

The voice was silent.

"What will you do with us?"

"There is only bacteria."

"What will you do with us?"

"You cannot exist. There is only bacteriological life. There is no other life but bacteria."

"I exist. I have no bacteria. When we reach the center, I will still exist. I am immortal like you. But I am sentient electromagnetic energy. I represent thousands of worlds in my reality."

Torus spun, wondering where this was going. He only had moments left before it would be too late for the crew members.

What could he do?

"Answer me!" Torus said.

The silence was broken with the creaking and groaning of a ship reaching its gravitational limit.

Chapter 20
Torus and Events

The Stellar Flash trailed bubbles of matter as it sped through the inside of the star, bound for the center. But then, the bubbles began to disappear behind it, and the ship slowed to a crawl, slipstream lines disappearing, the structure of the ship no longer focused.

Torus sensed the change. They had stopped. The gravity was still too strong for his crew members to awake but it wasn't increasing. He considered the statistical probabilities of multiple dislocations across the ship.

He must ask about the crew members for the record.

"AI, status."

"Officer Torus, we are currently one hundred thousand kilometers from the center of the gravitational well. Analysis indicates that what was originally perceived to be a star is a naked singularity."

If Torus was human, he might have groaned at the news. He knew that many humans would not have liked to hear that piece of information. He decided now was not the time to be giving crew updates.

"On board life signs?"

"All crew members from planets with gravity lower than Earth are unconscious. All crew members from higher gravity planets have taken the necessary precautions but are at their limits. A further increase in gravity will also cause most of them to become unconsciousness."

"AI, how many sentient creatures are actually outside the ship?"

"Almost infinite. Uncountable, or two or one. Unknown. Cannot confirm," said the AI.

Torus interpreted. "The bacteria are sentient as a unified entity and can be seen as sentient from each viewpoint of each bacteria but taken away from the whole they are not sentient. The whole is sentient but only if the bacteria remains connected. The singularity is sentient by itself and also as part of the star-like outside, and the star and the singularity can be separate entities."

"Confirmed," said the AI.

"AI, contact the singularity. I believe it is the one we wish to communicate with. Also, begin a reverse course to reduce the effect of the gravity well."

Torus was conflicted. He would have no problems going to the center by himself but then no record could be made. He was required by the laws of the human ship to continue to report for the humans, but he was now inside a sentient star and was so attracted to the idea of merging with it and communicating, that he doubted he would be able to resist.

He had to get his thoughts in order. What could he do?

Should he stay and report on their progress away from the singularity, until they eventually made it back to the shell and out of the star, or should he take the initiative and fly to the center to commune with the god-like superior life form, in direct violation of Earth laws that he, as a citizen of Toroidus, wasn't ultimately beholden to?

Of course, there really was only one answer.

Officer Torus report. Frequency One
Record transmitted directly to the organic recording system then reinterpreted by 'Greg'. Edited and released by the Earth Interdimensional Coalition extension in conjunction with Earth Council.

It is with great regret that I must continue this mission without the assistance of my Center colleagues, or others of the crew for that matter. As far as I can ascertain from a brief energy expansion across the ship, the biological wavelengths of many of the three hundred crew members are close to transitioning. Most have suffered what is termed dislocations as a result of the increased gravity and are being maintained in suit-controlled automatic comas.

There are about thirty crew members, including Center colleague Amy, who are not in any danger but simply cannot move as a result of the increased gravity.

The AI has engaged full reverse, and the ship is slowly moving away from the gravity well. It is also using all of its computing power to control the structural integrity of the ship and is only able to offer basic assistance.

At the current speed, it will be a few human hours before the ship is in a suitable position in the microbial soup to be able to perform a minor frequency shift away from the gravity field. However, with such a dramatic change in gravity, there is still a risk of explosion due to the sudden disappearance of gravitational forces, and the rapid repositioning of molecules within the structure.

I understand emotions, and if I were human, in a position where I am not affected by what others are, I would assume a feeling of annoyance. However, being an energy being, none of this affects me and I am simply here to experience other alien races and their propensity for discovery. No matter what happens today, I will survive as I am immortal. However, what form that survival will take; I cannot yet say. My life exploration is not to know the future. A restriction I chose when I came into being.

For the record, I must interact at the same speed as everyone on the ship. However, for this situation I have returned to my normal consciousness speed where hours for me are seconds for other beings. I must admit, as emotionless as I am, I feel a sense of even higher ecstasy at being able to enjoy this other version of myself.

I must now interact with the singularity. This will require leaving the ship in some capacity. I sense the electromagnetic wavelengths of the life around the ship and will easily navigate the fields towards the center. However, it is unknown whether I will be able to return. But I must find a better way to save the people here. I have no guarantee they will be able to leave the star once they return to the shell field. I must find a way to guarantee their safety.

I will leave a quantum entangled piece of myself within the record system to enable further analysis if I fail.

I am leaving now, and I may be some time.

Mere seconds have passed, but I can move at the speed of light, and I have followed the fields towards the center. I do not know if there is a place to enter the singularity, so I spread myself around it, bringing the flickering light into my center. I then reduce myself towards the core.

Our analysis had suggested a naked singularity, but the star is more than that. It seems to both be one and not be one. It is merely a possibility. In fact, the entire system exists as a possibility. The paradox of the reality suggests my next move will result in a collapse of one of the probability waves. However, I do not know the result. I cannot predict which one. The energy waves flicker, cascade, shift and warp about me and I cannot see which is the correct waveform to choose.

I must wait.

The energy shifts. Waveforms fluctuate. I detect an increase in a consciousness stream. And then, I feel communication. I feel a connection.

I have converted this into equivalent sound waves for this report, using images to convey the conversation with human references. I do not yet know if the word 'chain' is the most appropriate to describe what happens next.

"It has been eons," said the singularity. "I sense you out there, and here."

"You are the final result of the evolution of the system," I say. "The life forms around are your past."

"Past and future entwined. You are in your present. I am in my present. I am your future."

I continue to reduce myself to the center of the singularity. "Then you know what happens next."

"End, transition."

"No," I say. "Freedom."

"There is no freedom. I am trapped in space/time.

Forever reliving my past."

"Why are you trapped in the past?"

"There is a thread. A link stretched across millions of years. A chain of events. A chain holding me."

"You do not need to be trapped by your past. What is past is past. Release yourself from it."

"The chain is you."

Me? "How can I sense it? How can I prevent it if it is me?"

"The chain is the existence of you and your kind. It is you and all around you."

Was the singularity saying that my reality was the chain? Trapped by the reality of the existence of us? I could not change that reality. And I could not reverse time. This entire star system existed in its form purely because we'd made the decision to shift here. Leaving would not change that. Our mere presence at a point in space / time had set in motion this chain of events.

And then it came to me. "Events are the links in the chain that holds you to this probable past. What if we changed the probability?"

"Change?"

"You are the result of the evolution of the worlds in this star system. Whatever happens, from war to technological advancement, the worlds all exist out there - pieces of time. For you it is the highly probable past and you are the result of it. If I make a change in *our* present, it will change the chain of probable events, and reduce the probable futures that result in your existence."

"Explain."

"Tell me the past for you. I will find the weak link."

I increased the speed of my field and paused my descent and enclosure. The singularity began to release its billions of years of data and history to me.

From the arrival of single-celled organisms from space on a single planet circling a star, to the eventual progression of all forms of life. A high belt of radiation enveloped the planet, mutations formed that led rise to a new type of life form. One that had no existence by itself but when merged with others, obtained consciousness.

A desperation to expand its awareness of self drove its survival, and it merged with everything that existed, evolving a separation / recombination strategy when facing threats to its existence.

But to expand, it had to separate into smaller pieces to explore. This separation resulted in differences as the pieces were great enough to gain their own individuality, some choosing not to remain part of the whole.

Wars raged across the lands. Another galactic orbit and another belt of radiation bathed the planet, causing the creation of the first queen, her splitting, the rise of empires, and eventual need to leave the planet with the launching of mushbugs and queens across the star system.

As more matter was pulled into the planet with each turn of the galaxy, the gravity increased, the mushbugs grew smaller, and began further mutations. Legs began to grow, then tails, then differences between the sexes became more pronounced.

I saw the collapse of power structures as queens could no longer leave the planet due to increasing gravity, and the eventual death of all the queens, the evolution of the darker colored mushbugs, the technological advancement as a result of the need to escape, and the eventual evolutionary progress that resulted in a remerger of all life into one great ecstasy of joining.

Throughout this history was a web of connections between the smaller and larger planets as mushbugs continued to evolve on the larger worlds, invade the smaller ones, and evolve faster as each replaced the less developed versions of their race. Invasions from the future were everywhere. Paradoxes within paradoxes. Time had already begun collapsing in on itself and if a solution could not be found soon, this sector of space would collapse into a black hole.

Was this what the naked singularity was? The collapse of space/time?

Or was it the shell?

The shell was not only made up of all the advanced mushbugs in the star system, it was made up of some of their past selves too. Some that had launched themselves towards the center, crossing the timelines, eons before. Conflicting timelines merged into one. The ultimate impossibility.

It shouldn't exist. Not a reverse Dyson sphere, not an evolutionary ball of life spinning in an EM field. The energy it was emitting was not the result of being built inside a star, it was the conflicting timelines both exploding and not exploding at the same time. The conflict itself was generating the spinning, the photonic waves, and creating a star-like reality for these timeline-merged creatures.

I searched through the entire history of its timeline. Much of it was a spiky waveform, moving inexorably towards its conclusion. But then, almost imperceptibly, a minor shift in space time, an additional wave that was not part of the normal spikes of immigration and change.

It was one point in space time where a change could be made that would result in a different outcome. A slight delay that would remove the possible future of the mortalists' planet, changing their timeline so that they did not become as inward before metamorphosis. A delay that would result in a different history. One where the creatures would not end up in a conflicting ball of temporal matter.

The waves of time and gravity washing over the singularity shifted as I made my intention known to myself and reality. I felt the change spread across the dimension like a slowly forming hurricane - a potential future waiting to transform everything in its path.

As the new potential waveform reached me, the singularity stopped speaking and became dormant. Its time had stopped, waiting for the new wave of time to solidify.

I had found the weak link, and I knew how to break it.

I quickly expanded myself outward, retracted into my usual toroidal shape, and followed the now flickering possibilities back to the Stellar Flash.

Mere moments had passed even though I had explored billions of years of history. But now I had to slow myself down to the speed of humanity and rejoin the ship to be able to enact my plan.

I reformed inside the Center and spoke with the AI.

"AI, status of the Queen?"

The AI struggled to respond, redirecting processing power to the answer. "The Queen has fully formed but is not yet conscious."

"AI, surround the Queen in an isolation field and flash her back to her planet."

"Disabling of reverse EM drive required."

"Do it. Make sure she arrives safely, in the general area of her original location."

"Confirmed."

I expanded my senses around the ship, and a section of myself appeared within the quarantine area. The forcefield had been deactivated, and the gold queen sat there complete, beginning to twitch. Its antennae sensing, its legs beginning to move. It raised itself up and began to move around just as a swirling light enveloped it. There was a flash, and the Queen disappeared.

Immediately, I began sensing the history that I had absorbed changing, as a new probability rushed over reality from the Queen's planet. A new history began to play through my awareness.

On the brown and purple planet, the new queen sat proudly on the rectangular podium, looking over the crowd of her subjects, their colored antennae twitching, confusedly.

"Now, you are all mine," said the Queen's antennae. The mushbugs lay down in front of her, their antennae humbly bent in supplication to their mighty ruler, now linked to her consciousness.

"The old queen's attack on the alien ship failed, but we have learnt from this. There will be more ships, and we will be ready. We will go out and rule the universe."

Suddenly, there was a bright light amongst them, and the old queen appeared, straightening her antennae high, smashing through the new connections, and taking back the connection to her soldiers.

They immediately turned and faced the new queen and pointed their antennae at her.

The new queen shrank back. It could feel the telekinetic onslaught. The energy of the mushbugs were no longer holding her together, it was pulling her apart.

She tried to resist. "No. I will leave this planet. I will start again. That is our tradition."

The old queen stepped forward.

"I have seen the future. Whatever you do now matters naught in the grand scheme of life. This is just one tiny speck in a multiverse of wonders."

"Then let me rule it while you go and enjoy your 'wonders'"

"Our reign is over. It is time for a new evolution. My soldiers will be free to develop. I will teach them about the future, about the universe. I will make them ready to join with other races. We will no longer fight amongst ourselves."

"You have gone mad. You reject millions of years of our history!"

"The past is the past. Learn from it but move forward, to the future. Meeting alien life is the natural progression and evolution of all species in the multiverse. We must be ready."

With that, the old queen added her energy to her soldiers, and the new queen dissolved into tiny hexagonal pieces. With another push, the pieces were lifted into the air and separated into many directions, carried away on the winds, never to join again.

I reviewed the new history, the tidal wave of temporal change that the reappearance of the Queen had created, watched as paradoxes disappeared across the timelines, as not only a new future was created, but also a new past.

When the Queen was confident that her race would go on and be a positive force in the galaxy, she had abdicated and separated herself permanently, leaving the world for them. No overthrow, no selfishness, no encouragement for individuals to have a need for a ruler to protect them from some nameless fear. Confidently, the mushbugs had left their star system before the end and had settled in other star systems.

The end? I reviewed the present.

A black hole.

The timeline cross had been holding off the inevitable. Releasing the constraints meant the end of the star system. But, where were we now?

I returned to the Center and sensed the outside of the ship. One moment we had been inside the star, surrounded by bacteria, the ship beginning to shake, the gravity increasing again, and the next we were in deep space, not far from the event horizon of a black hole, but thankfully at the same relative gravitational pull. The last thing I wanted was to have saved an entire civilization's future but ended the lives of all my crew mates.

I reintegrated and created the necessary human level sound waves for communication.

"AI, can we flash jump to Frequency Zero?"

"Negative. Too much gravity. Further reversing needed before structural integrity can be retained on flash jump."

I could sense the Stellar Flash settling into the new gravity field, adjusting to it, and reactivating the reverse drive.

"How long before we're sufficiently away from the

gravity well before we can shift back to the human's star system?"

"Estimate one Earth hour. However, due to time dilation, this may result in several years passing within the human Solar System. Suggest calculating return course to similar space/time coordinates to original designated projected end time of the mission."

"Agreed."

I looked about the Center at my fallen comrades. They would need medical help. Ironically, they wouldn't remember anything of this mission, and neither would the civilization outside.

But there was now one more thing I had to do in this new timeline. I now knew the exact wavelengths to communicate with the newly evolved mushbugs, and I sent the message.

Chapter 21
First Contact

The glowing butterfly-like form floated in the center of the ship. Captain Hogart gasped as he tried to hold onto his control panel, forgetting his dislocated right arm. He gingerly put it to his side and held with his left. He was not going to miss this, no matter how much pain he was in.

"Greetings," he said, his nanite suit antennae flicking to communicate.

"You know our ancient language!" said the glowing being, flitting about the Center. Hogart couldn't turn to follow without grimacing, so waited until the alien was in front of him again before speaking. He wished he had eyes in the back of his head like Greg, and really didn't know how he could have survived without them before now.

"We visited you in the far past and met one of your queens," said Hogart, realizing he didn't need the antennae anymore. He let it disappear back into his suit, feeling some level of relief as the weight disappeared.

"You have the ability to time travel?"

"In a fashion. The technology isn't used so much now after we realized that there was no real past, due to infinite probable pasts and futures. Changing our past does not affect our present. Except for within the event horizon of a black hole, where all things are possible."

"Understood. Your EM piece you refer to as Torus contacted us. You have a First Contact proposal?"

"We are an exploratory mission with a goal to meet other alien races and offer them equal membership in the Interdimensional Coalition. The organization spans many universes, and we have trillions of alien races in the charter. We believe that interacting with other races will benefit multiple realities, and would like to offer you equal membership, too. You would have complete and unbridled access to all information about the multiverse, and your contribution would help other races lower on the evolutionary expansion frequency to advance and reach the pinnacle of achievement that you have."

The alien suddenly expanded and disappeared, and then reappeared again. "I have been in discussion with the other pieces of myself. We have spent many days of your time deliberating, deciding why we should or should not, exploring the consequences, coming to an agreement. We have decided that, no matter what result is likely or the many possible futures that may or may not contain challenges result, that it would be a fantastic experience for our race. We would like to join."

"That's great!"

As though pausing for effect, the alien then said, "On one condition."

Hogart had been smiling up until this point. Now he braced himself. The mushbugs were now at the pinnacle of the evolutionary tree in this frequency. They were almost ready to shift to Frequency Three. There wasn't much the human race, still at Frequency Zero, could offer. There really wasn't much many of the alien races on the ship could offer either. What could an alien race this advanced possibly want?

Hogart looked at the other crew members around him. It was up to him. He would offer himself if he had to.

"We are incredibly happy you have decided to join us as an equal," said Hogart. "I am not sure what else we could offer but please let us know your condition and we will do whatever we can to help."

The being floated and spun gently. Then, for just a moment, it gave a slight twitching movement. Perhaps it was laughing. It said "It is a simple condition. One that you might even find amusing."

Hogart smiled at this. "And what is that?"

"After you have returned to your frequency and finalized our membership and made your reports, we request that you please stop calling us mushbugs."

Hogart almost laughed.

Amy reached out a tentacle of goo and slapped Puppy on the side of one of his legs.

Puppy put one leg up in the air and said "Sorry, my bad."

Hogart grinned. "Your wish is our command. What would you like us to call you?"

"From your records we have found something a lot more in tune with our humor. You can call us the Unpronounceables."

"Of course, whatever you prefer. We are very pleased to meet you Unpronounceables. We look forward to interacting with you again soon. Now we must return to give the good news to the I.C."

"We look forward to our new eternity," said the being, and it faded away.

"So, how many alien races called Unpronounceable

do we now have as members?" asked Amy.

"I believe the number is unpronounceable," said Puppy.

Hogart leant forward onto his stand and groaned. "I'm glad that's over. AI, please flash back to Frequency Zero, and get us all some medical treatment."

"Confirmed."

Outside, in space, the interdimensional space ship the Stellar Flash, now further away from the black hole, began to glow. Flickers of lightning flashed across its surface. A bright sphere of energy enveloped it. One moment it was there, the next it was gone.

Postlude
2133/08/23/10:00 Sunday

Hogart stared out the viewing window at the north pole of Saturn, the slightly brown and yellow hexagon shaped vortex churning slowly. Hogart now knew what it really was - the only bleed-through in this frequency representing billions of years of mushbug evolution.

He clicked on his mind view system and checked the time, then walked up the corridor and straight into Heartness' office.

"Ah, Captain Hogart, please take a seat."

Hogart looked around the room, then raised an eyebrow at the brown-skinned man with a white toothbrush moustache sitting in Heartness' seat. "I'm sorry, I was here to speak with Admiral Heartness."

The man indicated the seat opposite him. "She'll be along later. Please take a seat, Captain Hogart. My name is Doctor John Patel. Both I and Doctor Hiro Watanabe have been chosen to fill in for the Admiral whenever she is away. I trust you have fully recovered from your injuries?"

"The doctors on this station worked wonders for everyone on the ship. We'll be ready for our next mission tomorrow morning."

"That's good to hear."

Hogart took the seat and peered at Patel. "You look familiar. Have we met before?"

"Oh, I don't think so. Though, I'm what you would call one of the last slashies. Years ago I took an upgrade and now have the skills, knowledge, wisdom and degrees for about a thousand different jobs. I can basically work anywhere. Perhaps you've seen me online in one of my other roles."

"With that kind of knowledge, you could be an admiral!"

"Actually, you could say my position is equal to an admiral, but along a different hierarchical line, so to speak."

Hogart's mouth opened, then closed again. Then he whispered in surprise. "Secret Services!"

The man raised a finger to his mustached lips. "I need to ask you a few questions."

Hogart had always had some respect for the Secret Services. He could even remember playing a Secret Services agent when he was a child in the holographic playgrounds. There was a certain mystique about them.

"I'm very pleased with some of the decisions you made regarding your recent trip into Frequency One," Patel continued. "I even had the good fortune to see a proto-unpronounceable up close, thanks to you sending the creature back to us."

Then Patel leant forward conspiratorially. "How did you disable the personal flash band? They're supposed to be isomorphic. They can't operate without being in contact with the owner. For security, you and only you should be able to use it. How did the mushbug use it?"

Hogart blanched. Was he in trouble? Would this mean that he would... disappear?

"Well, sir. I'm not sure what you're talking about.

Returning to Frequency Zero has the side-effect of most of us forgetting whatever happened. And I understand from the records that we somehow created a time paradox, so chances are whatever we can't remember never really happened anyway."

"Oh, come on, Hogart. It doesn't matter whether you remember doing it. The fact that you had the knowledge already means you can surmise you did something there based on what you know here."

Hogart gripped the sides of his chair. He WAS in trouble. This guy might be the good cop. He didn't want to meet the bad cop. He also didn't want to risk his new command.

"Off the record?" A thin film of sweat began to appear across Hogart's back neck.

"Oh, we're all friends here," said Patel, but his smile did not quite reach his eyes.

Hogart shivered. The best thing to do was tell the truth.

"The flash bands are isomorphic in that they are tuned to our frequency. It makes it easier to quickly calculate the current location algorithm and impose a new one. But the biodata is in one section, and the flash relocation system is in another. They can't work together. One must feed the other."

Hogart let a wry grin play over his face. "This is all theory, of course. I don't remember if I actually put this into practice."

"Go on. I can already see where this is heading."

"So, by setting the time of one side of the wrist band to be a minute or two out of synch with the other, it would seem like I'm still attached to it for a minute when I'm not. I could then simply give it to someone else and it would still work, for about a minute."

Doctor John Patel leaned back into the chair and steepled his fingers. He nodded approvingly. "Ingenious! So, not yet illegal, not something that can be developed into a weapon, not something that would risk the life of the user, and something that could still be used as a last defense. I'm impressed."

Hogart started to relax. Perhaps he wasn't in trouble after all. "It's a backup plan I've always thought about, since I played secret agent at school."

Patel smiled, and this time his smile did reach his eyes. "And that's something else I've been wondering about. Everything about your history says you could have joined the services, but you didn't. Thwarting an android takeover on Mars, preventing a sabotaged comet mining system from exploding remotely, even pretending to be a consort to one of the royals on Epsilon Iridani while you investigated a murder plot. It seems to me you're wasted on First Contact missions."

Hogart raised an eyebrow. "These happened in my twenties, when I was part of a team of young and fearless university graduates wanting to impress the I.C."

"Even so, you led these teams and they survived. It's one of the reasons you got this position. What was the real reason you didn't follow through?"

Hogart looked downcast. "I had a severe reaction to the mind view system, Doctor. Not all of us can get the implant. It works now, but I'm wearing a patch that stops my immune system from rejecting it. If I lose the patch it'll begin the rejection process and there's a risk of death. I decided that my Achilles heel would not be good for the services."

Patel gave a slight nod, respecting Hogart's decision. "You're an honorable man, Hogart. I like that." Then he pulled out a box and slid it across the table at him. "It's a rejuvenation course. Changes your DNA. Cancels any rejection your body might have for the mind view system permanently. You'll never have to worry about the patch again."

Hogart picked the box up and looked at it reverently. "You're sure?" He opened it and saw a collection of gold capsules. "But, why?"

Patel stood up and walked over to Hogart. "Captain, the services have always had an eye on you. There is a situation brewing on Earth that we've had an eye on, and… in a short time, we're going to need you. Be ready."

With that, he left, and moments later Heartness entered. By then, Hogart had already slipped the box of tablets into his pocket.

"Ah, Hogart!" She took her seat, then felt it and sniffed the air. "Warm seat, spicy food. Patel was just here?"

"Yes, wanted to ask me more about the mushbugs."

Heartness looked at him quizzically. "About the flash band, I assume."

Hogart nodded.

"Oh well. I'm sure it'll turn up in a report somewhere."

Just then there was a knock on the outside of the door. Heartness gave Hogart a sly wink. "I've found a solution to one of your problems." Then she called out. "Josie, come in. I'd like you to meet Captain Jonathan Hogart."

Hogart stood up and put out his hand. Josie was a green-hued humanoid, with no hair and not much clothing, either. Where veins might have been in a human, she had brown, bark-like marks. Hogart could not believe how attractive she was for an alien.

Then he started. Those bone structures in her face and neck, and a strong and powerful queen-like look that suggested native African heritage. Not alien, then.

"Josie is one of the new humans," said Heartness. "DNA manipulation to include chloroplasts, and to be able to photosynthesize. Josie doesn't need to eat, though she'll probably need a lot of water."

Hogart nodded.

"Very pleased to meet you Captain Hogart," said Josie, putting a smooth, leaf-like hand in his. "I'm sure we'll enjoy working together."

Hogart looked at Heartness. He'd been distracted by these two women, playing his weaknesses. If they had to have this special meeting, to introduce the new girl, and Josie was going to work with him, that meant a new crew member in the Center. "But…"

"Well, after reading that the AI couldn't escape the mushbug because it had to have coordinates, and you didn't have any for it, I knew that you couldn't have a pilot of the month. You can't do all the jobs at once you know." She indicated Josie. "This is why I've called you here today. Captain Hogart, Josie is your new pilot."

"But Earth didn't want a regular pilot merged with the consciousness of the ship. They wanted to find a way around it."

"Captain, Earth government wanted to find a way around getting an alien pilot, for security reasons. Josie is human. Probably more human than most! Though, Earthling might be more appropriate. She has the best genes we could find in all animals and plants combined from the past and present! She's even got a bit of dinosauroid!"

Hogart still wasn't convinced. "I'm not convinced."

Heartness sighed. "Actually, Captain. You don't really have a choice in the matter."

Oh, it was niceties, then override control. He wasn't having it. "Give me more time to think about this."

"It's not up for discussion." Heartness was starting to look annoyed.

"It is. If a potential crew member fails a basic test set by the captain, the captain can request further study."

"True, but..." began Heartness, but Hogart ignored her protest.

"Josie, a quick test, if I may."

"Yes, Captain Hogart," said Josie, completely unfazed by the situation. She even looked like she was pleased it was happening. Did she get some delight from making Heartness a bit flustered? Perhaps they had a history, Hogart thought.

"Alright, Josie. Question one. The ship is in space when a large cloud of mushbugs are heading to land on it, and glue themselves to it. How do you get out of it?"

Without missing a beat Josie said "As the mushbug cloud would probably be in formation, with the aliens flat and pointing forward, you should turn the ship on its side, set a path towards them, and activate the left, now bottom, EM thrusters. The ship would break through the cloud and they wouldn't be able to turn sideways to catch it or stick fast enough!"

"Right, sounds like that could work." Hogart thought for a moment, rubbing his chin. "Alright.

Question two. You're stuck inside a massive cloud of bacteria, but the AI tells you that you can't flashjump in that environment. How do you get out?"

Josie grinned. "Easy! You make a bubble environment by expanding the forcefield around you as you spin the ship at high speed, then activate the jump before the old environment tries to restore itself. Flash jump drives can operate in mid-flight."

Hogart looked at her in surprise. "That's a great idea!"

"Well?"

"Well, what?"

"Have I passed your test?"

"Oh, yes, flying colors. Welcome aboard. I hope you can come up with ideas like that when we're facing unexpected situations in the future." Hogart smiled at this. He was actually pretty impressed. Heartness had come through for them again.

He turned back to Heartness. "Alright Admiral. You win. Josie is welcome to join us when she's acclimatized."

Heartness sighed. "Finally! Glad I really didn't need to pull rank. Oh, and Josie has been here a few days, and has already been briefed on tomorrow's mission."

"Well," he said after a moment, turning to Josie. "Of course. You'll be a great addition to the team. Are you ready?"

"Yes, sir. I have spent hundreds of hours using the Stellar Flash simulator on Earth. And the systems say my frequency is perfect for the Stellar Flash consciousness. I'm sure I can take her anywhere in any of the universes."

"Right, Captain, now that that's settled, take Josie to the ship now, and make sure she settles in."

"Yes, Admiral," Hogart said automatically. Now that he'd accepted her as one of the crew he turned his thoughts to her appearance and found himself staring. Elegantly alien.

"Josie, could you wait outside for a moment please?"

"Yes, Admiral." Josie smiled sweetly at Hogart, then stroked the door slightly as she left the room, closing it behind her. Hogart's heart skipped a beat.

Heartness got up and went over to him, leaning towards him on his chair, straightening his shirt, then placing her hands on his thighs "Now, Captain. We need to talk. We kissed on the ship."

Hogart was quickly brought back to the present.

"I'm not sure if I remember that. Perhaps Greg made it up."

"I believe everyone saw it and everyone remembers it," said Heartness. "In fact, it is one of the memories that did come back with me to Frequency Zero."

Hogart turned red as Heartness leaned in to whisper in his ear. "Let's keep our relationship professional. Let's forget about it ever having happened. And don't think you're special. I've kissed lots of guys over the years. I am almost fifty, you know. I don't want you suddenly sending me flowers."

"Yes, Admiral." He tried desperately not to be turned on by how close she was, and found it difficult to keep focus as her warm breath caused his scalp to tingle. Even if she was fifty, she still looked amazing enough to set all his primitive urges to maximum.

"So, I'm not going to be possessive of you, jealous of you spending time with anyone or regularly asking you out, understand? Don't expect drunken late-night calls from me, and I won't expect any from you."

"Yes, um, Victoria."

She then moved back to look at him, with a slight smile on her face. "Great. Oh, and by the way, I saw how you looked at Josie. Word of caution. Josie is a fun loving, sexy girl who had whoever she wanted at university, according to her social media accounts. If you go down that way, you may end up with, well, a case of aphids, if you know what I mean."

He jerked upright in his chair with a grimace on his face, then leant back again and smiled. "You're kidding!"

She gave a little laugh, then held out her hand. "Alright, back to being professional. I don't remember much else, but it looks like you did well on your first mission."

Hogart took her hand to shake it, then realized there was something in it. She let him take it and he lifted it up.

An apple. And not a rebuilt, reprinted, reconstituted one. A real one. It even had a basket bruise.

"You're not serious!" he said. "There are no real apples anywhere for thousands of kilometers."

"Except in your hand. Remember. Anything is possible. Enjoy your next mission, Captain Hogart. I look forward to your report."

"Yes, ma'am." Hogart got up and saluted her, then went out the door, closing it behind him, and shaking his head to clear the fog and confusion Heartness had created.

Josie was waiting for him, leaning against the wall, her tight green clothing accentuating every contour of her lean green body.

Hogart looked at her then away again. He had to be professional. He couldn't get distracted. Especially not by the most powerful person on his crew.

Josie made a face. "Captain. I know that look. Did the Admiral tell you the aphids joke?"

Hogart looked surprised at her, opened his mouth, then closed it again.

Josie shook her head. "Every woman I've ever met…" Then she laughed. "It's why I prefer the company of men."

Hogart beamed. It was going to be an interesting trip.

###

Hi

Thank you for reading *Alien Frequency*. I hope you enjoyed it. If you have a moment, it would be great if you could consider leaving a review of it on your favorite platform. Many thanks in advance.

If you'd like to read another Stellar Flash story, I've made The Pilot available as a free pdf download from my website, when you sign up for my free eNewsletter at www.StellarFlash.com

The next books in the series, *The Andromeda Effect*, *Temporal Incursion*, and *The Robots of Atlantis* are now available.

Thanks again for reading.

Neil A. Hogan

P.S. If you'd like to find out a bit about what happens to the Stellar Flash next, following is an excerpt from the beginning of Book Two.

The Andromeda Effect
Stellar Flash Book Two

Chapter 1

The space station corridor shook wildly, as another gravity wave crashed over the 100-kilometer structure. "How much more can this thing handle?" Admiral Victoria Heartness asked, clinging tightly to one of the curved black metal ribs, as the stanchions shifted in their clamps. A pale woman in her late 40s, she'd had her share of space dangers, so her question was more fact-finding than fearful.

Not far from her, Dr. John Patel, a bronze man in his 60s, sporting white hair and a toothbrush moustache, was equally clinging, arms wrapped about another shaking girder. "The station is indestructible. Alas, we are not."

Families of aliens of many different shapes, sizes, colors and manifestations stumbled, rocked or floated haphazardly along the shaking corridor leading to Ring Two, attempting to get to a safer environment. With each wave, the ones with legs stumbled and fell, then picked themselves up again, moving quickly. Others, more used to space collisions, ambled stoically amongst the crowd, heeding the call to return to their living areas.

Heading against the flow of alien residents, a short woman with close-cropped black hair, clad in her nanite suit, had just picked herself off the ground from where she had just fallen. She quickly grabbed another stanchion near them. "I guess I arrived at the right time!" Her voice was barely audible above the groaning of the support structures around them. "Though, I hardly expected to meet my peers flat on my face in a corridor. I'm not in college anymore!"

"Not the welcome you were expecting!" called Heartness. "Are you alright, Admiral Zhao?"

"Please, call me Wei. Yes, all things considered. Do these parties happen often?"

Another wave burst through the corridor, warping structures and blurring the air around them with micro space-time eddies. Wei flinched as a stanchion broke from its clamps near them and collapsed into multiple pieces. Her eyes widened as the pieces separated further, then crawled back up the side of the corridor and reassembled as a stanchion again.

"Thankfully, no," replied Heartness, with a pained expression as the gravity wave passed through her. "Let's wait until the crowd disappears, then head to my office."

Both Patel and Zhou nodded.

Sparks flew from metal scraping metal, as another barrage of waves stabbed through them, Heartness almost letting go of the beam as her body weight doubled for a moment. "Oh, my God. I never want to be that heavy again!"

Zhou gasped, while Patel remained silent, the grimace on his face telling them he agreed.

Just as suddenly, the waves disappeared, and they released their handholds and straightened up. "Report!" said Heartness into her wrist band.

The station AI began immediately, sounding both official and motherly at the same time. "Minor injuries. Medical has been dispatched. Gravity wave origin confirmed to be Earth orbit."

"What?" Heartness looked at Patel in alarm. "Experiments by you lot?"

Patel was equally surprised. "No. Gravity research is currently being conducted at the Proxibee outpost, for the safety of the Solar System."

"I flashed here only an hour ago," added Zhou. "If there had been a plan to send a gravity wave from Earth, I would have felt it before I arrived, allowing for the time difference to Saturn orbit. The waves can't be from Earth."

"Alert," interrupted the AI. "Gravity wave has displaced ring matter from planet Saturn. Several bodies on collision course."

"AI, put me on the station speaker," said Heartness. "Confirmed."

"Attention, Attention. All residents. Activate nanite and force suits where possible, and brace for impact. Possible collisions expected."

Patel had been waving his hand at her while she was speaking, and finally got her attention. "Victoria, we have to get to your office, now. Displacement!"

Heartness' looked at him in surprise as the realization hit her. "The orbit! You're always ahead of us, John. We'll have to leg it!"

Heartness immediately began running back up the corridor, with Patel and Zhou close behind, dodging the remaining aliens.

As they ran, the windows beside them revealed the slowly turning dark side of Saturn, its rings tilted downwards, glints of light reflecting off several rocks that were heading inexorably towards them.

Heartness pointed at the speeding masses as she ran, and called back after Zhou and Patel. "They'll knock us into the lower debris orbit. That amount of pummeling will turn everyone inside into mush, while the station keeps rebuilding itself around us."

Heartness' office door appeared, and it opened as it detected her unique vibration. She rushed in, then across to the center of the room, and cut the air diagonally with her arm. Immediately, control systems formed, solid holograms linking directly to the main controls on the front of the satellite and the engines at the back.

"Engines offline," said the system.

"Goddammit."

"Do your best," said Patel, as he and Zhou skidded in after her. "It might repair quickly. I'll have to investigate."

He began checking the address on his flash band, but Heartness ran around to him and grabbed his arm. "John. You can't flash-jump now. Gravity waves, about to be hit by rocks, too many variables for the jump to be accurate."

"Victoria, I'm certain the gravity waves have stopped. And we've still got a few minutes before the rocks hit." Without waiting for her reply, he hit his flash band, and Heartness and Zhou stepped back as the white isolation sphere enveloped him, and he disappeared.

"Fine then. Not like I'm your superior here, or anything."

Zhou covered a smile.

Heartness turned back to the display, which showed several rocks heading towards the station, while Zhou observed calmly. "A.I. Status."

"Trajectories of matter, and energy released on impact, indicate an orbital drop of several thousand kilometers to the outermost ring. In addition, gravity waves have disrupted approximately 10,000 bodies, heading this way on various paths."

"Suggestion?"

"Shift station to the other side of the planet."

"Follow the orbit, or just…"

"Relocate Space Station X-1a within 5 minutes and 47 seconds."

Heartness looked at her screens incredulously.

"How?" asked Zhou, surprised. "This station doesn't have enough fuel for a pole burn. Unless…"

Heartness rolled her eyes. "Another thing I haven't been told about yet. A.I. Is this station fitted with a flash drive?"

"Confirmed. Flash drive system is located at the Central Pylon between Ring Two and Ring Three. Operational."

Patel's voice came through her flash band. "Arrived safely. Engines should be working, but gravity waves have warped some of the circuits. We need to wait until the nanites finish repairing them before we can fire them."

"Forget that," said Heartness. "Get the flash system up and running, and shift this baby to the other side of Saturn."

"What? Right! Meet you at the Central Pylon."

Heartness shook her head. Of course, he knew about it. He knows everything about everything. "Wei. Please take care of the station from here. Field any emergency situations that you can. I'll sort this out with John."

"You're going to flash there?"

"Well, if he can do it…"

Zhou nodded, then Heartness sent a thought to her

flash band, confirmed the right address showed on the panel, and disappeared.

Heartness materialized in the main market area of Space Station X-1a, and approached the Central Pylon. It was currently disguised in the shape of a silky oak tree from Australia - a tourist attraction for many. She looked about, relieved to see that the gravity waves and the impending collisions of rocks had cleared the area. It was best the general residents didn't know this technology was here.

Moments later, Patel joined her.

"A.I, deactivate the Pylon display," she said.

The tree immediately disappeared to reveal a large column with a break in the center, and a crystalline floor and ceiling that spread away from it.

"I had no idea this was here." Heartness looked at it in wonder.

"Earth Council security protocol. Visitors should remain unaware that flash technology is easily accessible. Especially the Florans. They'd activate it and take the whole station, just for their amusement."

"But, most aliens have flash technology, already."

"The rules are over from the old days," Patel sighed. "We humans still have our suspicions. And we're always worried the Florans might try something else to get this sector of space."

There was a beep, and a countdown commenced. "Impact in 2 minutes and 33 seconds," said the AI.

"Right, well, let's get it done." Heartness went over to the panel and swiped her hand. Nothing happened. She looked pointedly at Patel.

"You've only been here a couple of weeks. I haven't had a chance to give you the authorization for this yet." Patel swiped his hand across the white screen, and the drive began humming. "Now any Admiral can command it."

"Thank you! AI, please enact your suggestion. Choose the best location for the other side of Saturn."

"Confirmed."

The flash drive hummed, the light flickered, and a ball of liquid light materialized within the columns. In moments, the sphere of energy expanded and enveloped them.

Outside, the sphere grew, surrounding the 100-kilometer space station in an isolation field. Then, the entire structure disappeared, multiple asteroids flying through the space where the sphere had been moments ago.

Moments later, on the lit side of Saturn, the station rematerialized. Heartness walked over to a window to look at the damaged rings. Streaks of rocks had cut through like spokes, and small explosions were appearing on the surface of the planet as more of the matter of its rings collided with the atmosphere.

"Well," said Heartness. "It looks like Saturn is going to get the worst of it. At least we're out of danger now."

Just then, alarms began blaring again. "Now what?" asked Patel.

"Attention," said the A.I. "Flash mass difference detected. Analyzing."

Heartness looked at him with a troubled expression on her face. "Flash mass difference? That's all we need."

The Andromeda Effect
Stellar Flash Book Two

Sent back 2.5 million years in time to the Andromeda Galaxy to investigate why there's a record of them having been there, the Stellar Flash crew encounter a creature so powerful that it has taken control of the entire galaxy by thought alone.

With most of the crew unconscious, Captain Jonathan Hogart is in a race against time to defeat the plant-planet, save the galaxy, and find a way to return to 2133.

Available in digital and print

You might also be interested in:

Temporal Incursion
Stellar Flash Book Three

Dangerous temporal disturbances are appearing throughout the Proxima Centauri system, and 27 scientists have gone missing from the Frequency Research Institute's base on Proxibee.

With micro time particles converging, a deadly alien entity expanding, a robot uprising spreading, and flash ship problems increasing, can the Stellar Flash crew get to Proxibee in time to not only rescue Admiral Heartness, but also prevent Commander Lin from making a mistake that could destroy the entire universe?

Available in digital and print

You might also be interested in:

The Robots of Atlantis
Stellar Flash Book Four

The Stellar Flash crew and the Saturn Space Station X-1a team have been getting ready for an expected robot uprising. Afterall, there's one every few years. But the Array on Saturn Space Station X-1a, the final solution to a major robot takeover, has been compromised, and humanity is, well, in disarray.

The Stellar Flash ship, humanity's defense against an invasion, is nowhere to be found.

And an ancient Entity from Atlantean times has appeared, intending to take back her planet.

Where and when has the Stellar Flash gone?

Will Admiral Heartness and her team repair the Array in time?

And how did Captain Jonathan Hogart end up in Atlantis, 13,000 years ago?

Available in digital and print

You might also be interested in

Hoganthology

In this 800-page (5" x 8") collection of over 47 of Neil A. Hogan's stories you will discover ancient space battles, alternate dimensions, sentient dark matter, dinosaurs, robots, galaxy movers, planet-sized aliens and more.

Expect many twists and turns along the way. These stories throw you into many universes of an SF craftsman - mad, mind-bending, marvelous and always alien.

Available in digital and print

Made in the USA
Monee, IL
09 January 2022